FIERY BLIZZARD

E.D.G. SMITH

CHAPTER 1
FIRE!

Friday, 19 November 1880: Audrey opened her eyes and slowly sat up. She brushed the hay off her coat and looked around the dark barn. Something wasn't right. "Brad, wake up," she said.

"I'm awake," he said, reaching down from the top bunk to touch his sister's shoulder. "What is it?"

"I think I smell smoke."

"Smoke?" questioned her brother, sitting up and sniffing the air. "I smell it, too."

Both of them threw off their blankets and quickly put on their boots. Blaze and Ebony nickered and pawed the floor of the barn.

Brad opened the tack room door and yelled, "Fire! The house is on fire!"

Falling snow muffled the sound of breaking glass as Vasya Petrov smashed a chair through the bedroom window of his burning house. Brad and Audrey ran through the blizzard toward the blaze. Flames engulfed the front of the house and were racing across the roof by the time Brad and Audrey reached the bedroom window.

"Help Olga!" screamed Vasya through the broken window. Smoke snaked around Olga, then shot upward once outside as she struggled to climb out.

Brad and Audrey helped Olga through the broken window. As soon as Vasya saw that his wife was free, he dove headfirst through the window into the snow. His long johns were smoking, as was his hair. Flames pursued him out the window, like evil hands trying to pull him back into the inferno from which he had just escaped.

"Your hair!" shouted Audrey. Releasing Olga, she threw herself on Vasya's smoldering head, pushing it into the snow.

Brad cupped his hands, scooped a mound of wet snow, and pushed it under Audrey onto Vasya's still smoldering hair.

"Vasya!" screamed his wife. "Vasya!"

"I not hurt," assured Vasya, rising to his hands and knees.

"We've got to get away from the house," said Brad as windblown firebrands swirled around them, hissing as they fell into the snow. "Thank God the wind isn't blowing the fire toward the barn."

Vasya stood up and tenderly wrapped his arms around his wife.

"Vasya, we almost die," whimpered his shivering wife, the snow swirling around her bare feet.

"Mr. Petrov," urged Brad, "let's go to the barn. It will shelter us from the blizzard."

Vasya carried his wife to the barn. Audrey brought a couple of empty feed bags and wrapped them around Olga's feet. Brad picked up an old horse blanket from a peg on the tack room wall and wrapped it around Olga's shivering body.

"Thank you," said Olga. "My shoes in house with clothes."

The four of them stood in the tack room doorway watching flames devour the house. Their faces flushed from the heat of the fire as their backs shivered from the cold wind whipping around them. Tears streamed down the Petrovs' faces as the flames slowly subsided.

"Olga," consoled Vasya, his arms around his wife, "we live. We not die in fire."

"Is winter now," said Olga. "We no have money. We no have food. We not live long."

"You won't die," insisted Audrey.

"We'll go to Bevins' general store first thing in the morning," said Brad. "We'll get you some shoes and clothes."

"Reverend Wesley will help too," added Audrey. "The church will help you."

"You not understand," said Olga. "Church not help. You see."

The four of them gazed at the burning embers of the house through the subsiding blizzard. A sudden gust of wind blew a clump of snow from a tree onto the smoldering remains. Little puffs of steam accompanied the sizzle of melting snow.

Brad lit the tack room lantern, and said, "Audrey, when I put the horses in the barn last night, I think saw a jacket. Help me take a look for it."

They searched around the barn and found the jacket Brad had seen earlier, as well as a pair of old boots.

"Here, these should help," offered Brad, handing them to Vasya.

"Thank you." Vasya put on the jacket. "Barn jacket. Barn boots. I wear when work in barn."

"The tack room will provide shelter until morning," said Brad. "Then we can go into Riverton."

"They need clothes or blankets," reminded Audrey.

"Horse blankets," sniffed Brad, picking one up. "They may smell like a horse, but they'll at least keep you warm tonight."

Audrey held the lantern as her brother picked up Blaze and Ebony's saddle blankets. Returning to the tack room, Brad put the blankets on the bunk for the Petrovs.

"Brad and I have our long underwear and coats," Audrey assured Vasya. "We'll sleep in the hay. You and Mrs. Petrov can share the bunk in the tack room. Mrs. Petrov, the burlap bags should help keep your feet warm. While you're getting settled, Brad and I will fill a couple of empty feed bags with hay to cover you. That with the blankets should keep you warm until morning."

When Brad and Audrey returned with the hay-stuffed feed bags, the Petrovs settled into the bunk. Vasya wrapped his arms around his wife and they huddled together beneath the blankets. Olga sobbed as Brad covered them with the bags of hay. Brad and Audrey quietly left the tack room as Vasya soothed his wife in their native Russian language.

"Brad," whispered Audrey, "it's terrible. Their house is gone; they have nothing."

"True," agreed Brad, "but we'll take them to the general store first thing tomorrow morning. We've got to get them some clothes as soon as possible. Between Mr. Bevins and Reverend Wesley, we'll get the Petrovs through the winter. Right now, we've got to get ourselves settled for the night."

Audrey held the lantern while Brad got their saddles and put them in the hay bin. Together, they leveled the hay in front of their saddles and spread a few empty feed bags on top of the hay.

"It's fortunate that Vasya had these empty feed bags," said Brad as he filled one with hay.

"They'll help keep us warm tonight," said Audrey. "A bag of hay isn't as good as a blanket, but with our long underwear, we'll be okay."

When they had stuffed four bags with hay, Audrey laid down and pulled two of the bags on top of her. Brad blew out the lantern and hung it on a large peg. When his eyes adjusted to the dark, he crept to his new bed. Feeling for his saddle, he laid down and covered himself with the other bags of hay.

"Good night, Audrey," said Brad, tugging up his coat collar.

"Good night, Brad," replied his sister.

Saturday, 20 November 1880: The rooster's crow woke Brad. He reached over and touched his sister, "It's time to get up, Audrey."

"Brad," she muttered groggily, "did I hear a rooster?"

"Yes," he said. "It's the Petrovs' rooster."

The fire, the Petrovs, the barn, and the blizzard abruptly came to the forefront of Audrey's thoughts. As she slowly sat up, she saw that Brad was brushing hay off his clothes.

"I hear the Petrovs stirring," said Brad. "As soon as they're up, I can get our blankets to saddle the horses."

"That isn't going to be very long," said Audrey. "I can hear his boots on the floor now."

"Morning," greeted Vasya, coming out of the tack room. "I thank you for saving our lives."

"Yes," said Olga. "Thank you. We have no house, but we have barn, livestock."

"I'm glad we were here to help," said Brad.

"Now, we need to get you some clothes," said Audrey.

"You right. We hitch horse to wagon for trip to town," said Vasya, his arm around his wife.

"I'll get the harness while you get your horse," Brad told Vasya.

Several minutes later, the Petrovs' horse was harnessed and hitched to the wagon. Brad saddled Blaze and Ebony while Audrey and Vasya put the bags of hay on the floor and seat of the wagon to help keep the Petrovs warm.

"We're ready," said his sister, standing in the barn doorway.

Brad led Ebony and Blaze out of the barn while Vasya picked up his wife and carried her through the snow to the wagon. Shivering from the cold, she clutched the blanket tightly around herself as she settled down into the bag of hay. Vasya climbed into the wagon seat, and Audrey wrapped a second blanket around Olga's legs and feet, topping the blanket with another bag of hay.

"We go," announced Vasya, slapping the reins on the back of the horse.

Before mounting their horses, Brad and Audrey

watched the wagon move past the snow-covered ashes of the house.

"This is terrible," Audrey said, gently nudging Blaze to a slow trot. "Their house, their clothes, their furniture, all of it is gone." She paused for a moment and then continued, "They lost everything except the barn and the livestock."

"They even lost the new blankets and supplies that we delivered for Mr. Bevins yesterday," said Brad.

"But not the long johns," said Audrey. "Vasya wore them last night, or he wouldn't even have had them today."

"And Olga wouldn't have her old blankets that she gave us when the blizzard forced us to sleep in their barn last night, either," added Brad.

The ride to Riverton went swiftly with the morning sun's warmth melting the snow on the road. The wagon and horses sloshed their way down Riverton's Main Street.

Just after Mr. Bevins opened the general store, Vasya parked his wagon in front and helped his wife down. Brad opened the door for the Petrovs who hurried into the warmth of the store.

"Come with me to the stove, Mr. Petrov," invited Audrey. "You're freezing."

"I not want to die," said Olga as her husband put his arms around her and walked with her to the stove.

"We not die," said Vasya assuringly. "We live. We still have barn."

Tears streamed down Olga Petrov's face. Her fearful eyes darted to Mr. Bevins.

"Mrs. Petrov," exclaimed Mr. Bevins. "What's wrong? Why should you die?"

"Our house burn last night; we now live in barn."

"That's terrible," replied Mr. Bevins. "Were you able to save anything?"

"We save ourselves," recounted Vasya. "Fire very fast; kitchen all flames. We leave through window."

"You have no shoes," said Mr. Bevins, staring at Olga's burlap-wrapped feet. Looking more closely, he saw that only a blanket covered her flannel nightdress. Vasya was clad a little better with a pair of old boots and his barn jacket covering the top of his long underwear. Pink scalp showed where his hair had been singed.

"I'll get you some clothes and blankets," declared Mr. Bevins. "First, however, how about some hot coffee and a sandwich?"

"Thank you," said Olga, smiling for the first time since the fire.

Mr. Bevins went to the stove, poured two cups of coffee, and handed them to the Petrovs. Then he reached under the counter and brought out a flour sack with some sandwiches and apples.

"Roast beef sandwiches," he said, handing them to the Petrovs.

"But that your lunch," protested Vasya.

"True, but now it is your breakfast," Mr. Bevins insisted. "My wife and daughter will be arriving with their lunches later this morning. I'll share with them; my wife always packs too much food anyway. Please, eat and enjoy."

He turned away from the Petrovs, looked at Audrey and Brad, and murmured, "Audrey, please ask Sheriff

Tate to come right away. Brad, see if Reverend Wesley can come, too."

"Yes, sir," said Audrey, heading to the door.

"I'll take Ebony," said Brad. "The reverend and I can ride double on the way back."

Minutes later, Audrey burst into the sheriff's office only to find it empty. She had just decided to head back out when the door behind her opened, startling her.

"Audrey, I saw you rush in. What can I do for you?"

"The Petrovs' home burned down last night," she told the sheriff. "They're at the general store now. Mr. Bevins asked me to bring you right away."

"Let's go then," he said, holding the door open for her.

While Audrey and Sheriff Tate were heading to the general store, Brad had dismounted from Ebony and was knocking on Reverend Wesley's door.

"Why, Brad," welcomed Mrs. Wesley, "what can we do for you this fine morning?"

"I came for the reverend; is he in?" asked Brad.

"He sure is," hollered Reverend Wesley, coming out of the kitchen. "I trust there hasn't been another stage holdup."

Reverend Wesley was referring to a recent stagecoach holdup by the Badger Gang. Brad, Audrey, and their father had been passengers on that stagecoach.

"No holdup, but there was a fire," responded Brad. "The Petrovs' home burned down last night. They're at the general store right now, and Mr. Bevins is supplying them with some clothes and blankets. He asked me to come get you."

"Sounds like the church can help them. Let me grab my coat, and I'll be right with you."

"I brought Ebony," said Brad. "We can ride double to the general store."

Brad mounted Ebony and then took his foot out of the left stirrup. The reverend used the empty stirrup and mounted behind Brad. Brad gently pulled the reins to the left and clucked to his horse. They rode down the street toward the general store, arriving a few minutes after Audrey and Sheriff Tate.

"Morning, Reverend," nodded the sheriff.

"Morning, Richard," replied the reverend. "Let's go see what we can do to help."

"Brad," said the sheriff, "please go to the livery and bring my horse. Bring the reverend's horse, too. I think we're going to take a ride out to the Petrovs'."

When they entered the general store, they saw Mr. Bevins talking to the Petrovs. Reverend Wesley noticed the burlap bags wrapped around Mrs. Petrov's feet and the long johns under her husband's barn jacket.

"Brad said your home burned down last night," said Reverend Wesley. "It must have been bad. Can you tell me about it?"

"It happen fast," recalled Vasya. "Fire everywhere. We climb out window."

"A fire usually gives you more time than that, but not always," remarked the sheriff. "Did you hear anything just before the fire?"

"I hear glass break, but Vasya no hear," said Olga.

"Breaking glass," noted the sheriff thoughtfully. "Anything else unusual? Did you smell anything?"

"Maybe kerosene, I not sure," said Olga.

"Brad, Audrey, did you hear anything unusual?" Sheriff Tate inquired.

"Something woke me up, but I don't know what," answered Audrey. "After I woke up, I smelled smoke, and then heard the tinkle of glass as Mr. Petrov broke the bedroom window so they could escape the fire."

"Let's ride out to your place," the sheriff told the Petrovs. "I'd like to have a look around."

"I not want to make trouble," appealed Vasya. "You stay. No need to come."

"It's my job, and it's no trouble," the sheriff assured him.

"Vasya, you can borrow my horse and ride out with the sheriff," said the reverend. "I'll get some additional supplies and follow in the wagon with your wife."

"We have no money for supplies," protested Vasya, buttoning his new overalls.

"That may be true," said the reverend as he handed a new jacket to Vasya, "but when someone around here experiences a tragedy, like your fire, folks help each other. Just like you did in the search for Harold Benton, we're here for you."

Outside the general store, Brad looped the reins of the three horses over the hitching rail. Audrey was waiting for him at the door.

"What did the sheriff say?" asked Brad, stopping outside the store to confer with his sister.

"Not much. He's going to ride out with Vasya and look at what's left of their house. Reverend Wesley is going later in the wagon with Olga and some more supplies. I'll be helping them load the wagon. Let's go inside."

"I see you're back," said the sheriff as Brad closed the door. "Are the horses outside?"

"Yes, sir."

Reverend Wesley quickly strode across the store to Sheriff Tate and Vasya. "Vasya, my horse is outside. Why don't you take it and go with the sheriff? I'll follow with your wagon."

Vasya started to object, but Sheriff Tate interrupted him. "Come with me, Vasya. We need to leave now."

Sheriff Tate put his hand on Vasya's shoulder as they departed. Brad and Audrey watched them mount up and start down the street at a slow trot.

"Brad," called Mr. Bevins, "please go over to the hotel and give this note to Mr. Acker. Wait for his reply, and then bring it back to me. Audrey, will you please help Mrs. Petrov select the right pair of shoes while I help my other customers?"

Brad slid the note into his pocket and hurried down the boardwalk. When he reached the hotel, he crossed the lobby, stopped in front of the door marked <u>PRIVATE</u>, and knocked twice.

"Who is it?" inquired Mr. Acker.

"Brad Benton, sir; I have a note from Mr. Bevins."

"Come on in, Brad."

David Acker was sitting behind a large mahogany desk that held an inkwell, a ledger, and a kerosene lamp. The bright sun was shining through the window onto a rather large sheet of white parchment that Mr. Acker was examining intently.

"I was just checking the hotel's Thanksgiving menu," he said as he walked around the desk to greet Brad.

"Mr. Bevins asked me to bring you this note."

"Thank you," said Mr. Acker, reaching for the piece of paper.

He stroked his chin thoughtfully as he read. "Brad, have a seat."

Brad sat down as Mr. Acker pulled a thick decorative rope hanging from the wall and returned to his desk. He opened a drawer and withdrew another ledger. He had just lifted the ledger's cover when the side door to his office opened.

"Yes, Mr. Acker?" inquired a waitress.

"Sally, the Petrovs' house burned down last night. They lost everything and spent the night in their barn. I'd like you to pack a box with some food: several loaves of bread, some meat, rolls, a pie, whatever you can quickly put together that doesn't require cooking. Take the box to the front desk, and Brad will stop by in about ten minutes to pick it up."

"I'll start on it right away," she said, turning to leave. "Brad's name will be on the box when he comes to get it."

"Thanks, Sally. I'll have the reply for Mr. Bevins in a minute, Brad," said Mr. Acker.

He dipped his pen in the inkwell and wrote a brief note. When he finished, he rolled a blotter over the paper. He repeated the process after he wrote a check to go with the note. He opened another drawer to retrieve an envelope and inserted them into it.

"This is the reply for Mark. I've included a check to Bevins' General Store. I know he didn't ask for it, but tell him a box of food will be ready before the reverend arrives with the wagon. And Brad," added Mr. Acker, his eyes twinkling as a smile spread across his face.

"Yes, sir?" said Brad expectantly.

"Thanks for bringing the note. You've been a big

help. Now hurry back to the general store, and say hello to Reverend Wesley for me. Please come back to get the box afterward."

Brad took the envelope and left the hotel. He thought to himself, *I've never seen Mr. Acker at church, yet he's always friendly with Reverend Wesley. I wonder why he doesn't come to church."*

Brad entered the general store and halted briefly to let his eyes adjust to the dimness of the unlit store. Mr. Bevins was behind the counter, and his daughter, Wilma Sue, was across the store helping a woman select some cloth. Brad quickly walked up to Mr. Bevins and gave him the envelope.

"That was pretty fast," remarked Mr. Bevins.

"Brad," said Reverend Wesley, coming out of the back room, "will you help me load this box into the wagon?"

"Yes, sir."

Brad picked up one end of the box, the reverend the other, and they carried it across the boardwalk, lifting it up and onto the back of the wagon.

"Reverend, Mr. Acker said to say hello. He said you didn't ask for it, but he's preparing a box of food for the Petrovs. It will be at the front desk with my name on it."

"That's a very kind thing for him to do. Can you come with us to the hotel? If I know David, I'll need your help with that box, too. It will be a large one."

"Of course," replied Brad. "I'll help you at the hotel while Audrey gets the supplies Nana wanted."

"Olga," called Reverend Wesley, "Are you ready?"

"Yes, Reverend, I ready."

Reverend Wesley and Brad helped Olga climb up to the wagon seat. Once they were all in, the reverend gently slapped the reins and headed to the hotel. When they arrived, Brad jumped down and went to the front desk.

Moments later he returned to the wagon. "You were right, Reverend, it is a big box. I'll need your help."

"David is a generous man," replied the reverend, climbing down from the wagon. "Let's get that box loaded. There's a lot to do today."

The two of them heaved the box onto the back of the wagon. It was filled with several loaves of bread, some cheese, apples, a pie, and a cloth sack of roast beef.

"There's even a butcher knife, cups, plates, spoons, and forks," observed Brad.

"That's David," said the reverend, climbing back into the wagon. "Thanks for your help, Brad. I'll see you at church tomorrow." The reverend gently slapped the reins, and the wagon lurched forward. Brad looked intently at the wagon as it disappeared past the curve on the snowy street. When he could no longer see it, he started back to the general store. As he entered, his sister turned from the counter, a cloth sack in her hand.

"I've got everything on Nana's list," she said. "Let's go home; I'm ready for breakfast."

Brad looked at her for a moment before answering. "Uh, right, let's go home."

They mounted their horses and started down the street. Audrey looked at her brother as they rode out of town; he stared ahead, oblivious to his surroundings.

"Brad." He didn't respond, but continued riding, deep in thought. "Brad," said Audrey again, this time reaching over and gently poking him in the ribs.

"What?" jerked Brad, glancing at his sister.

"What are you thinking about? Did something happen at the hotel?"

"No, I was just thinking about Reverend Wesley and Mr. Acker."

"Well," prodded Audrey, "what about them?"

"Mr. Acker doesn't come to church. Mr. Bevins writes him a note, and Mr. Acker writes a check to the general store." Brad paused, took a deep breath, and continued. "Mr. Acker also gives a big box of food to the Petrovs and asks me to say hello to Reverend Wesley. When I tell the reverend about the box of food, he says it'll be a big box and asks me to come help him load it into the wagon. He acts like he's a close friend of Mr. Acker."

"So?"

"Well, it was a big box. It was a big wooden crate heaped with food and kitchen supplies. I don't understand."

"Don't understand what?"

"Why he does that for total strangers. He doesn't come to church, but he and the reverend act like they're old friends. It just doesn't make sense."

"I see what you mean," Audrey said as they dismounted and led their horses into the barn. "But helping people in need is part of being a Christian."

"Yes, but so is going to church."

"Yes, it is."

"Do you know something about Mr. Acker that I don't know?" asked Brad.

"I don't think so. Maybe we'll learn more in church tomorrow. We can ask Jake Jackson, if he's not too busy. He seems to know just about everything about everyone in Riverton."

"Good idea," said Brad. "But first, let's eat breakfast and tell Ma and Nana about the fire."

CHAPTER 2
THE ARSONIST

Sunday, 21 November: It was a clear, crisp morning, and the sun glistened on the snow that had fallen during the night. The town folks were walking to church, and those from the country were busy hitching their wagons and buggies to the posts beside the church. Brad and Audrey stood in front of the steps to the Riverton Community Church, chatting with a group of their friends.

"That's right," said Audrey. "The Petrovs' house burned down Friday night. They're living in the barn now. Mr. Bevins gave them some clothes and blankets Saturday morning."

"They're new to Riverton," added Wilma Sue. "They arrived just before Mr. Benton was taken by Duke Badger. My Pa says they're from Russia."

"Reverend Wesley talked with Mr. Acker and my pa about the fire last night," said Wilma Sue. "Pa said that the reverend would make an announcement about it this morning."

Old Man Abbott turned the corner and walked toward the church while Brad, Audrey, and their friends discussed the fire. When the old man started up the church steps, Brad turned to him and said, "Good morning, Mr. Abbott."

"To all of you, good morning, too," he replied as he entered the church.

"Ma's just started the prelude," said Audrey. "We'd best get seated."

Brad, the first up the steps, held the door for Audrey and their friends. Seeing Reverend Wesley and Sheriff Tate conversing softly in the corner of the narthex, he waited a moment, hoping for a chance to speak with Sheriff Tate. When his mother finished the prelude, he knew there wasn't time, so he hurried down the aisle and squeezed into the pew beside his sister.

"What kept you?" she whispered as their mother played the introduction to the first hymn.

"I wanted to speak with Sheriff Tate, but he was talking with the reverend. I heard a little bit of what they were saying," he replied.

"You were eavesdropping!" hissed Audrey in dismay. "Well? What did they say?"

"I couldn't hear too well, but it was about the fire," replied her brother.

The congregation started singing the first verse without much enthusiasm, but Reverend Wesley quickly changed that. His powerful voice boomed from the back of the church, encouraging folks to sing with a little more verve. He strode down the aisle on the second verse and took his place at the pulpit. After he led the opening prayer, a deacon read the lessons and the gospel.

"Good morning," the reverend began, "I usually make announcements after the sermon; however, today I'll make a few beforehand. First, I'd like to share some good news with you. Father Trevor O'Brien will be arriving in Riverton next week. His bishop is sending him to Riverton to establish a Catholic Church. We are growing and can certainly use another church. I'll tell you more about it next week. Now, the bad news; there was a fire Friday night. A family new to Riverton was burned out. They're living in their barn with a few clothes and blankets that Mr. Bevins gave them. They have no stove as it was damaged in the fire. Accidents and fires happen, but many can usually be prevented. Sheriff Tate informed me just before the service that the fire that destroyed the Petrovs' home Friday night doesn't appear to have been an accident."

There was a murmuring of "oohs," and an "I'll be," and similar phrases from the congregation. Folks looked around at one another, and some shook their heads in disbelief while others nodded in agreement.

Reverend Wesley left the pulpit and walked up to the front row of pews. He looked at the congregation, smiled, and said, "We're going to have a house-raising next Saturday. Jake Jackson will be the leader. I want every member of this congregation to see Jake and let him know what you can give to the Petrovs. If you can give some clothes, bedding, kitchenware, or food, it's needed. Bring what you can to Jake as soon as possible. David Acker has already made a generous contribution to help get things started. Mark Bevins provided a set of clothes and ordered a cook stove, a stove to heat the house, and other building supplies Saturday morning. We need to get their house built in one day, and that day will be next Saturday. After all the hard work, everyone deserves some fun, so we'll have a dinner and dance at the school that night to celebrate."

There were smiles and grins as friends pondered about the food they'd be bringing to the dance. Things quieted down, and folks redirected their attention to the reverend.

"That," said Reverend Wesley, "is what Christianity is about. That is what the church is about; helping the poor, helping those in need, helping your neighbor, and loving your neighbor. Whoever burned down the Petrovs' house wasn't thinking about loving them. They were thinking about hate. Hate destroys people, particularly the haters themselves."

Reverend Wesley surveyed his congregation, returned to the pulpit, and began his sermon which grasped everyone's attention. Through the simple act of asking them to help the Petrovs, Reverend Wesley offered the congregation an opportunity to perform a small act of true Christianity. Many citizens of Riverton would have assisted the Petrovs without the reverend's request. Even though some had already helped, his sermon still touched their hearts.

"Abby, the closing hymn please," said the reverend.

As soon as the hymn was over, folks started leaving while Mrs. Benton played the postlude. Audrey turned to her brother and muttered, "I can't believe that someone would deliberately set the Petrovs' house on fire. How horrible; they could have been killed!"

"Just like the reverend said in his sermon, whoever set that fire is full of hate," Brad responded.

Wilma Sue joined them and said, "Pa gave the Petrovs food and blankets." She paused, and then continued. "Brad, Audrey, you saw them. They didn't even have enough clothes to keep warm. The sheriff told the Petrovs that Reverend Wesley would announce their needs in church this morning, but Mrs. Petrov said the reverend wouldn't do that."

"Why did she think the reverend wouldn't help them?" asked Audrey.

"Pa asked her the same question," Wilma Sue continued, "Mrs. Petrov said that when the reverend realized they were Jewish, he would change his mind."

"What's that got to do with the reverend helping them?" asked Brad.

"Harry Acker and his father came to the store yesterday afternoon," said Wilma Sue. "Mr. Acker told me that the Petrovs are from Russia where Jews are treated poorly. Many have been forced to leave their homes, and some have even been killed just for being Jewish."

"That's not right," protested Audrey.

"The early Christians were treated that way by the Romans," Brad reminded them. "The same went for some Negro slaves in this country. Many slaves were abused and even killed by their owners. Hatred, bigotry, and discrimination based on skin color, religion, education, the country you were born in," Brad paused for a moment, "that's wrong. People should be accepted for what they do for the town, their community. That's what Reverend Wesley says we should do. He says that's Christianity."

"Brad," said Wilma Sue with a smile, "you'd make a good preacher."

Before Brad could respond, Mrs. Bevins and Mrs.

Benton joined them. "Edith," said Mrs. Benton, "let's iron out what we're doing for Thanksgiving."

"Well, I'll make the roast and bread like we discussed," offered Mrs. Bevins.

"We'll bring the pies and vegetables," said Mrs. Benton. "What time should we arrive?"

"How about noon?" suggested Edith Bevins. "We'll plan on dinner for two o'clock."

"Good. Now that that's settled, we'd better tell Reverend Wesley that he outdid himself with his sermon," declared Abby Benton as she took her friend's arm and headed for the door.

Wilma Sue noticed the reverend talking with a young man. "It looks like there's a new man in the congregation."

"Who's that?" asked Audrey.

"The one talking with Jake Jackson and the reverend," said Brad. "He's got black hair, and is about the same height as Jake."

"We'll find out who he is soon enough," said Audrey. "Jake's bringing him over."

"Brad, Audrey, Wilma Sue," introduced Jake, "this is William Brock. He's new to Riverton and will be coming to our church."

"Pleased to meet you," said William as he gently took Audrey's and then Wilma Sue's hands.

"Welcome, Mr. Brock; church is a good way to get to know the people of Riverton," said Brad as he shook William's hand. "Are you working anywhere yet?"

"I'm working at the livery right now," he replied. "I'd like to start a ranch next spring."

Mrs. Bevins came over, put her hand on her

daughter's arm, and whispered, "I'm sorry to interrupt, but we've got to be going."

"I've got to go," said Wilma Sue, turning to join her mother. "I'll see you next week, Mr. Brock."

"Excuse me," said Brad. "I'd better get the buggy. Nana's raising her right eyebrow at me."

"It was a pleasure meeting you, Audrey," said William, bowing slightly before he turned and left the church.

"Seems like a right fine young man," remarked Jake. "He even volunteered to help build the Petrovs' new home next Saturday."

"Audrey," called Nana from the door of the church, "Brad's here with the buggy."

"I'm coming. Goodbye, Mr. Jackson."

The Bentons had Sunday dinner when they returned home from church. Later that afternoon, Brad and Audrey finished up their homework while their father read a new book; their mother and grandmother wrote some letters.

Their grandmother, Victoria Hanson, came to Riverton just after the Benton's house was built. Brad and Audrey called her Nana. After sandwiches and pie for supper, Brad and Audrey were putting away the dishes when their grandmother turned to her son-in-law.

"Harold P. Benton," she announced, "it's been three and a half weeks since you were shot by Duke Badger. You're working full days now and have put on some weight. How do you feel?"

"Quite a bit better, thanks to your cooking and Brad and Audrey's tracking and medical skills. I thank

God they found me and fixed me up before the wolves got me."

"We knew we'd find you, Pa," said Audrey, refilling her father's coffee cup. "We couldn't let Duke Badger win."

"Thanks to your uncle, Marshal Henry Benton, and his team of U.S. Marshals, that despicable monster is no more," Victoria said.

The family recalled the stagecoach that had been held up by the Badger Gang four weeks earlier. Duke Badger had become so angry when he discovered that the strongbox was empty that he shot the driver and took Brad and Audrey's father as a captive. Sheriff Tate and his posse had searched for the gang unsuccessfully. When the sheriff returned empty-handed, Brad and Audrey packed up and headed out on their own to search for their father. They found the Badger Gang's trail, followed it, and on the second day they found the gang's campsite.

Just as a blizzard was coming in, Duke shot and wounded their father, stole his boots and coat, and then abandoned him to the wolves. Brad and Audrey shot four wolves, bandaged their father's wound, and built a shelter as the blizzard swept over them. On their way home, they captured a member of the Badger Gang, brought him to Riverton, and turned him over to Sheriff Tate.

"Let's not dwell on that evil monster anymore," said their mother. "Come; sing next week's anthem with me."

She played the hymn, "Old Hundred," once, and then the Bentons sang the first verse. Mrs. Benton stopped and said, "I think it's a little slow. Let's do the second verse at a faster tempo."

After the second verse, Brad said, "That tempo does feel better. I don't like it when hymns are played slowly."

"Brad," his father began, "I've been thinking about the Petrovs' fire. Let's check our stoves and stovepipes. We don't want our house to burn down like theirs."

"But Reverend Wesley said the fire didn't look like an accident," recalled Audrey.

"True, but he didn't say it wasn't one either."

"Whether it was an accident or not, I don't want our house to burn down, Pa," said Brad. "Let's check the stovepipes."

Brad went out to the barn and brought in a stepladder. He placed it under the parlor stovepipe and climbed up. "It looks tight, Pa, and there's no rust, either."

"Good. Let's check the kitchen next."

Brad moved the ladder into the kitchen, set it under the pipe behind the stove, and climbed up as he had in the parlor. "This one's tight, too, Pa."

"I'm glad to hear that," sighed their grandmother. "Blaze and Ebony are nice horses, but I have no desire to live in the barn with them."

"Me neither," laughed Brad. "I'll fill the wood boxes, and then I need to do some more studying before school tomorrow."

An hour later, Brad closed his books and started up the stairs for bed. Audrey put down her book and followed him up. When they reached the top of the stairs, she put a hand on his arm. "Brad, do you think whoever set fire to the Petrovs' house will do it again to anyone else?"

"Yes," said Brad. "I do."

CHAPTER 3
THANKSGIVING

Thursday, Thanksgiving Day, 25 November: The sun was bright, the air was still, and frost still covered the ground. Inside, the Bentons were just about ready for breakfast. Brad carried a platter of pancakes, and Nana took a plate of bacon and eggs to the table. Audrey poured the coffee while her mother filled the teacups. In a few moments, everyone was seated.

"Harold," nodded Mrs. Benton.

Harold Benton said grace, and everyone began filling their plates.

"It looks like it's going to be a real pleasant day," said their mother. "It'll be a nice ride to the Bevinses."

"Ideal weather for Thanksgiving," Nana agreed.

"But still brisk enough to work up an appetite for Thanksgiving dinner," reminded their father.

"I'm going to start on my appetite right after breakfast," said Brad. "The kindling buckets are just about empty."

"We've all got chores to do this morning," noted Nana. "This is going to be a busy household."

After breakfast, Mrs. Benton stood up and went to the kitchen. "I'll start the vegetables. We'll be leaving in a few hours."

"The pies are ready," said Nana. "I baked them yesterday."

There was a flurry of activity as they got the table cleared, dishes washed, kindling split, and vegetables prepared. Mrs. Benton and Nana dressed in their Sunday-go-to-meeting clothes. Brad saddled Blaze and Ebony while Mr. Benton hitched his horse, Ginger, to the buggy.

Brad was climbing the stairs to his room when he heard Audrey call him.

"Brad, how does this look?"

He entered her room as she twirled around in her new dress. It was light blue with a fitted waist and a lace collar. Brad suddenly realized that his sister wasn't just a girl anymore. "It, it looks nice, real nice," said Brad. "You'll be asked to dance a lot Saturday night."

"You really think so?" she asked, her face brightening.

"Yes," insisted Brad. "You look-—you look different. You're still my sister, but, well," he paused. "You just look different. You look older, more mature. I bet William Brock even asks you for a dance."

"Really? He's very handsome, well-mannered, and nice. Too old for me, but he is nice."

Before Brad could reply, their mother entered the room. "That is a lovely dress, Audrey, but you can't wear it if you're going to ride Blaze to the Bevinses."

"I know. I was just showing it to Brad," replied Audrey. "I'm going to change now."

"Me, too," said Brad as he left for his room.

Brad polished his boots, quickly put on his good clothes, and went back downstairs. His father had just picked up the small wooden crate with the pies and vegetables.

"Brad, would you get the door for me?"

"Yes, Pa."

After putting the crate on the floor of the buggy, his father turned and put a hand on Brad's shoulder. Looking into his eyes, he said, "Brad, I want you to know that I'm very concerned about the fire at the Petrovs'. If the fire was set by an arsonist, there may be more fires. We need to be alert at all times. You must tell me if you see someone looking at our house. Listen for strange noises at night, and be aware of anything out of the ordinary."

"Yes, Pa."

"It's time to be going. Let's see if the women are ready," said his father as they went back to the house.

Mrs. Benton, Nana, and Audrey were in the kitchen putting on their coats. "I've banked the fire in the kitchen range," said Nana. "It'll help keep the chill off the house while we're gone."

"It's going to be cold in that buggy," said Audrey. "I brought the quilt from the guestroom to keep you warm."

"Thank you," her mother replied. "We'll probably need it when we return tonight."

"I see everyone's ready," declared their father, entering the kitchen. "The pies and vegetables are in the buggy. Let's get going."

"Audrey and I'll give the house one last check," said Brad. "We'll meet you at the corral."

Brad and Audrey checked to ensure that nothing that could burn was close to the stoves. "The parlor is safe," said Brad.

"So is the kitchen," added his sister. "Let's go."

They closed the back door and headed to the corral. Their parents and Nana were already in the buggy. Their father gently slapped the reins, and Ginger started at a nice trot.

"Do you think there's an arsonist?" asked Brad as they walked to the corral.

"Yes," said Audrey, "but I can't even guess who it could be, or why they set the fire."

"Me either. Maybe we'll hear something at the Bevinses."

Audrey put her foot in her stirrup and looked at Brad. "There has to be a reason. No one sets fire to someone's house for the fun of it."

"Not if they're sane," replied Brad as he mounted Ebony. "Not if they're sane."

Brad looked down the trail to see the buggy turning onto the road to Riverton. Ebony and Blaze snorted and bobbed their heads.

"They want to race," said Audrey. "Shall we?"

"On the count of three," said Brad as he gently pulled back on the reins. "One! Two! Three!"

They released the reins. Blaze and Ebony bolted forward at a gallop, each trying to get ahead of the other. Ebony was ahead by a length when they reached the road. Brad and Audrey slowed the horses to a fast trot.

"Either Blaze is getting faster, or Ebony is getting slower," remarked Brad. "The last time we raced, Ebony won by two lengths."

"It could be that Ebony is slower. You have grown quite a bit the past few months," teased Audrey.

"So have you," replied Brad.

"Just what do you mean by that?" snapped his sister, her eyes flashing angrily.

Brad turned to his sister, astonished by her anger. Then it dawned on him that she had misunderstood him. "Audrey, what I meant is that you're growing up. When you showed me your blue dress this morning, I realized that you were, well, more mature."

Audrey's anger quickly subsided as she realized the true meaning of her brother's statement. "Thank you, Brad. I'm sorry I snapped at you."

They were gaining on their parents in the buggy, so Audrey slowed Blaze to a somewhat slower trot. Brad and Audrey chatted about the upcoming house raising for the Petrovs.

Sometime later Audrey said, "The Bevinses' house is just ahead. Let's get there first so we can help Nana out of the buggy."

They gently kicked their horses to a fast lope, reaching the Bevinses' homestead well ahead of the buggy. They dismounted and put their horses in the corral. By the time the buggy arrived, they were ready to help their mother and Nana down.

"Thank you," said their grandmother as she stepped down. "I'm not so old that I need help getting down, but it's nice to have it."

"Thank you, Brad," said his mother as he helped her as well.

"Welcome," called Mr. Bevins from the back porch of his house. "Happy Thanksgiving!"

"Happy Thanksgiving to you, too," responded Mrs. Benton.

"Audrey!" exclaimed Wilma Sue, picking up her skirt and rushing to her friend. "You're finally here."

"Wilma Sue has been checking out the window for the past hour," said her father. "It should be quieter now."

"That's right," agreed Mrs. Benton. "They'll keep to themselves."

"I'll take care of Ginger, Pa," said Brad. "I'll be in shortly."

"Thanks, Brad," replied his father. "I'll take in the box with the pies and vegetables."

Mrs. Benton and Nana were talking with Mrs. Bevins at the back door; Audrey and Wilma Sue were already in the house. Mr. Benton and Mr. Bevins took the box into the kitchen and stood on the back porch talking while Brad un-hitched Ginger.

"You've really grown," remarked Mr. Bevins when Brad joined them. "You must be a half-foot taller than last year."

"Just about; I'm five inches taller than I was last Thanksgiving."

"It's Victoria's good cooking that does it," said Mr. Bevins.

"Catching robbers and chopping wood helped too," added his father.

"If he keeps that up, he might become president someday," said Mr. Bevins.

"He just might do that," said his father.

"Speaking of presidents, what do you think about the election?" Mr. Bevins inquired.

"I'm pleased that Garfield appears to be winning," said Mr. Benton.

"The Electoral College will vote the will of the people, unless something happens."

Brad was astounded and said, "You mean the Electoral College could elect someone that the people didn't vote for?"

"They've always voted with the people in the past," explained his father. "They probably will this time. It is an odd provision, but the framers of the constitution created the Electoral College to protect the people."

"Each state sends a representative to Washington with instructions on how to vote," said Mr. Bevins.

"It protects the people, the country, from swearing in a president that was improperly elected," Brad's father continued. "There are a few men who will try to twist the election rules to get their candidate elected. They will shout about one law, rule, or piece of the election process to draw your attention from all of the other election laws and the whole election."

"That's lawyering," joked Mr. Bevins. "A good defense lawyer can convince a jury that a guilty man is innocent."

"And, a silver-tongued prosecuting attorney can sway a jury to convict an innocent man," countered Brad's father. "That's why the Electoral College serves an important role in our nation. They have time to study the Constitution and the Bill of Rights, and they determine the true will of the people based on the vote of the people. The U.S. is a republic, not a democracy. Each state, depending on its population, gets a certain number of electoral votes."

"The president is elected by the number of electoral votes, not by the number of people voting for him," said Mr. Bevins. "The creators of the constitution established the Electoral College system to keep a few populous states from controlling who was elected president. I hope the Electoral College won't be misled by the newspapers and the loudest voice from one of the political parties."

"True," replied Mr. Benton. "Maybe the Electoral College will be eliminated in the future, when the country is larger. Then the vote of the states, or even the congressional districts, could directly elect the president."

Brad, his father, and Mr. Bevins stood on the back porch, continuing their discussion about the election. Inside, the ladies were preparing dinner and talking about the Petrov house-raising that coming Saturday and of course, the dance afterwards.

"Wilma Sue, would you please ask the men to come in for dinner?"

"Yes, Ma."

Audrey opened the back door and Wilma Sue stepped onto the porch. "Pa, Mr. Benton, Brad, Thanksgiving dinner is ready."

"I don't know about you, Mark, but I'm ravenous," said Mr. Benton.

"My stomach's been growling for hours," Mr. Bevins replied. "How about you, Brad?"

"I chopped wood before we came, so I'm definitely ready to eat."

"Brad's hungry enough by now to eat the hooves off the horses," teased Audrey, standing in the kitchen door.

"Then we'd better let him in the house first. We have to save the livestock," quipped Mr. Bevins.

In a few minutes, the men had washed up, and everyone was seated. The table was really two tables; the kitchen worktable and the dining table had been pushed together and covered with a long cloth. Brad half-straddled the joined table legs. He and Audrey shared a bench, and Wilma Sue sat on the kitchen stool while the adults sat on chairs.

As soon as everyone was settled, Mrs. Bevins said, "Mark."

Mark Bevins bowed his head and said grace, thanking the Lord for the food, friends, and their warm house. When he finished, Mrs. Bevins announced, "Reverend Wesley stopped by the store yesterday. He said the Petrovs were having Thanksgiving dinner with the McTavishes."

"David Acker sent Jake out with a small stove and stovepipes," said Mrs. Benton. "They installed the stove in the tack room."

"That should keep them warm until the house-raising," said Mrs. Bevins.

"Reverend Wesley told me that when he drove up with the clothes, food, and other items the church had collected for them, tears came to Mr. Petrov's eyes," said Mr. Bevins. "He didn't believe Sheriff Tate at first, but he does now."

"That's good," said Victoria. "There should be no place in Riverton, or anywhere in the United States, for hatred and religious bigotry. We've all got to do everything we can to stop it."

"It looks like we've just about won that battle in Riverton," said Mr. Benton.

"That may be true," remarked Mr. Bevins, "but Brad is winning the food battle."

"Brad Benton!" exclaimed Audrey. "You've already eaten all your dinner."

"I have not," protested Brad, feigning indignation. "I've just eaten my first plate of dinner."

"Well, at least the horses are safe," Mrs. Bevins laughed. "Audrey tells me she has to guard the horses to keep you from eating their hooves."

"They're safe for now," said Brad, helping himself to another slice of roast beef and some beets. "The turkeys, too, since we don't have any around here."

After dinner, the Bentons and the Bevinses discussed the house-raising and how Riverton was growing. Mr. Benton pulled out his large pocket watch, looked at the time, and then slipped it back into his vest pocket.

"That certainly was a delicious dinner," he said.

"It sure was," agreed Mr. Bevins.

"We'd better be going," said Mr. Benton. "I'd like to get home before dark."

"It must be later than we thought," said Mrs. Benton, looking out the window. "It's getting dark already."

"Hmm, it's only five o'clock," murmured her husband, checking his pocket watch again.

"There's a big storm coming," said Victoria. "The snow is already falling."

"The wind is picking up too," said Mr. Bevins. "It looks like a blizzard."

The two families crowded around the parlor window

and watched the swirling snow and dark grey clouds to the west.

"You'd best stay the night," warned Mrs. Bevins. "It's not safe to go out in a storm like that."

"Our house isn't that big, but we can certainly make room for everyone," said Mr. Bevins.

"Brad and I can sleep on the parlor floor," offered Audrey. "It will be warmer than it was when we brought Pa back last month." She remembered finding their father after Duke Badger had shot him and left him for the wolves. Sheltering in their lean-to during the blizzard was tough, and the ride home was long and cold.

"Abby, Harold, you'll be in the guestroom," said Mrs. Bevins. "Victoria, you can share Wilma Sue's new bed."

"It even has a down quilt that my grandmother made," said Wilma Sue.

"Well," replied Victoria, "I haven't slept under a new down quilt for many years. This will be a treat."

"Then it's settled," said Mrs. Bevins. "Everyone has a place to sleep tonight. Would anyone like some more coffee or tea?"

"Tea sounds lovely," said Victoria.

"Yes, it does," agreed Mr. Benton.

"That's right," said Mrs. Bevins. "Mark said you developed a preference for tea after Brad and Audrey rescued you from Duke Badger."

Mr. Bevins looked at Brad and Audrey and said, "Brad, I understand you and Audrey did some fine shooting. Shot some wolves from about 400 yards."

"It wasn't quite that far," denied Brad, "but it was a good distance. I was afraid I might hit Pa."

"We just did what Pa taught us to do," said Audrey.

"We took our time, adjusted for the wind, and gently squeezed the trigger."

"It was a long distance," her father insisted. "The next morning, they showed me where they were when they had shot the wolves. It was the top of a small rise, well over 200 yards away. With the crosswind and the snow, the Lord must have been helping them; He had to be."

"We were so scared," said Audrey.

"That's right," Brad confirmed.

"That shows what good training can do," said Mr. Bevins. "You did as you were trained, and you hit your target. The Lord steadied your hands so you could shoot straight, just as your Pa taught you."

"Coffee and tea are ready," announced Mrs. Bevins. "Who wants coffee?"

Wilma Sue and her mother poured the drinks. The familiar serenade of stirring spoons crescendoed and then subsided.

"Brad, I don't want you chasing the horses for a midnight snack," chided Mrs. Bevins. "How about a roast beef sandwich?"

"Now that you mention it," said Brad, "that sounds wonderful. Thank you."

"Brad," said Audrey, "I know you chopped wood this morning, but I'm still amazed at your appetite."

"He'll have that appetite for at least another five years," their grandmother assured her. "Then it will taper off."

For several more hours, they talked about food, Duke Badger, and the election. The wind howled and the snowflakes swirled through the air like they were dancing.

"We'd best be getting to bed," said Mr. Bevins. "I've got to open the store tomorrow, and you folks will have a challenging buggy ride through all this snow."

Brad woke up. He didn't know the time, but it was still dark outside. He peered out the parlor window; the snow continued to fall. *I've got to go to the privy*, he said to himself. Quietly, he rose up and put on his boots and jacket. The room was chilly, so he opened the wood stove and added another piece of wood to the fire.

Audrey heard the noise, and by the light of the fire saw her brother. "Brad," she whispered, "it's not morning yet. What are you doing up?"

"I've got to go to the privy," he said softly. "The fire was just about out, so I added some wood."

"Wait for me," she said reaching for her boots. "I'll go with you. I know I won't be able to wait until morning."

"It's still snowing, so bundle up. The fire should be roaring by the time we get back."

They tiptoed to the kitchen door. Brad grasped the doorknob and started to turn it.

"I hear something!" Brad whipped open the door.

"Brad?!" cried a man whizzing past the back porch on a horse.

CHAPTER 4
THE ARSONIST STRIKES AGAIN

Midnight, Thursday, Thanksgiving night, 25 November: Brad and Audrey heard a *'whump,'* and then the porch was aflame.

"Fire!" shouted Brad.

Audrey raced to the stairs and screamed, "Fire!"

Brad grabbed a bucket, put it under the kitchen pump, and began pumping. "Please don't make me prime you," he pleaded, "not now."

The pump poured water into the bucket. Audrey came running with another bucket for her brother.

"Brad, let me pump. I know I'm not strong enough to throw water up to the top of the house; you'll have to do that."

"Just keep pumping," he shouted grabbing the full with one hand and placing an empty bucket under the pump spout with the other.

Audrey grasped the pump handle with both hands. She pushed it to the top, started pulling it down, and then jumped up to use her body weight to force the water up the pipe, out of the spout, and into the bucket.

Mr. Benton and Mr. Bevins clambered down the stairs two at a time. The women were right behind them.

"The back porch is on fire!" shouted Audrey, jumping up to leverage her weight on the pump handle.

Brad swapped buckets and ran out the back door. He turned and sloshed the water onto the side of the burning house.

"I'll get some shovels from the barn," hollered Mr. Bevins. "Edith, get our clothes and take them out the front door, then the furniture."

Mr. Benton and Wilma Sue cupped their hands and flung snow onto the raging flames while Mr. Bevins went to the barn and got some shovels.

"Harold, Wilma Sue," panted Mr. Bevins, running up to them. "Take a shovel."

The three of them shoveled snow and dirt against the burning backside of the house while Brad drenched the flames with buckets of water. In a few minutes, the fire was out. Wisps of smoke curled upward through the falling snow.

"We did it!" whooped Mr. Bevins. "The fire's out!"

"Let's get inside," said Victoria. "We'll catch our death of cold standing out in the snow like this."

"I'm freezing," chattered Wilma Sue.

In a few minutes, everyone was huddled around the parlor stove. Brad and Audrey stood back so the others who were in just their nightclothes could get warm.

"What happened?" asked Mr. Bevins, warming his hands over the stove.

"Audrey and I got up to go to the privy," explained Brad. "As I was opening the back door, I heard something. A man on horseback galloped past, and then the back porch caught fire."

"Mark," asked Mr. Benton, "who dislikes you enough to set fire to your house?"

"I don't know," replied Mr. Bevins, shaking his head. "I just don't know."

"If you'll excuse us," interrupted Brad as he leaned his shovel against the back porch. "Audrey and I'll be back in a few minutes. We really need to use the privy now."

"I've got the fire going in the kitchen range," said Mrs. Bevins. "Let's get our clothes changed. Then we can clean up the kitchen and back porch. Coffee and hot chocolate will be ready by the time we're through."

They looked at the wooden kitchen floor, a mess of muddy water, rocks, and dead grass. The boards on the back porch were covered with snow, dirt, and ice. The fire had blackened the backside of the house, and it was splattered with patches of muddy snow.

"I've lit three lanterns," said Victoria wrapping a scarf around her neck and buttoning her coat. "One for the kitchen and two for the back porch. Audrey and I will hold the lanterns on the porch while you men do the shoveling."

Audrey, her grandmother, and the men went out the back door to get started. Mrs. Benton swept most of the muck off the kitchen floor onto the back porch. Mrs. Bevins followed with a mop while her daughter wiped the counter tops and table. When the floor was finished, she hung up the mop to dry and sat down with Mrs. Benton and Wilma Sue.

Soon the kettle began to emit a low whistle. Mrs. Bevins glanced at the kitchen range and said, "It's too early for the train, so it must be the kettle. I'll make the coffee and hot chocolate. Wilma Sue, would you please set the table?"

"Yes, Ma."

"I'll make some sandwiches," offered Mrs. Benton.

Outside, the men were removing the dirt and snow from the porch. Brad used a hoe to gently scrape the muddy snow off the side of the house. All the muck was mounded beside the garden fence.

"That will keep the broken glass in one place," said Mr. Bevins. "I'll be able to bury it next spring after it thaws; I don't want anyone to get cut."

Mrs. Bevins hollered out the back door and said, "Coffee, hot chocolate, sandwiches, and pie are ready when you are."

"I'm ready for that," said Mr. Benton.

"Especially Victoria's apple-blackberry pie," noted Mr. Bevins.

The men had washed up and were sitting down by the time Brad and Audrey returned from taking the shovels and hoe back to the barn. The two stood at the kitchen sink and washed the soot and dirt from their hands and faces. When they finished, they sat down with the others.

"That was quite an experience," said Mr. Bevins. "I feel like a cat that just lost one of its nine lives."

"I'm glad you stayed the night," her husband told their guests. "We couldn't have put out the fire without you."

"Pleased we could help," Mr. Benton assured him. "We were fortunate that we caught it in time."

"The next time we invite you over for dinner, we'll try not to have a house fire," chuckled Mrs. Bevins.

"Brad," asked his father, "did you hear or see anything unusual?"

"Well," said Brad, "just after I opened the door, the man shouted my name."

"Shouted your name!" exclaimed his grandmother.

"That's right," said Brad.

"It sounded like the man was surprised to see Brad," Audrey commented.

"Apparently, the rider stuffed a rag into a whiskey bottle full of kerosene, lit it, and then threw it against the back porch," their father informed them. "I can still smell the kerosene."

"That explains the broken glass," said Brad. "But couldn't the bottle have exploded before the rider threw it?"

"Yes, he was lucky" said his father. "The rider probably lit the kerosene-soaked wick with the end of a cigarette or cigar, immediately kicked his horse to a gallop, and hurled the bottle as he passed the porch. It was vital that he threw it right after lighting it. Holding a bottle of kerosene with a burning wick for more than a few seconds is extremely dangerous; the bottle could have exploded in his hand. That's been discovered by many rioters, to their sorrow."

Brad ate the last bite of pie on his plate, looked at Wilma Sue's mother and said, hopefully, "Mrs. Bevins, may I please have another piece of pie?"

"You certainly may," she replied. "And if you tell me how you made the pump work so fast, I'll bake you one of my special pumpkin pies. I have to prime that pump most of the time."

"Thanks," Brad grinned as she put another piece of

pie on his plate. "I pumped hard and fast and then Audrey took over. At first, I thought I might have to prime it, but then I felt the water coming. Fortunately, the valve was still wet. Most likely, the valve is about worn out. If you replace it, you shouldn't have to prime it so much."

"Mark," said Mrs. Bevins, "can you bring a new valve home tomorrow night? I'll put it in Saturday morning."

"Well, folks, that rooster is going to start crowing as soon as the sun comes up," said Mr. Bevins. "We'd better get some sleep."

The dishes were washed and stacked, and everyone went back to bed. Brad and Audrey took off their boots, pulled up their blankets, and tried to go back to sleep.

"Brad," whispered Audrey, "are you still awake?"

"Yes."

"I think we can figure out who set the fires," she said. "Do you want to try?"

"You know I do, or you wouldn't have asked me."

"Well, it's just possible that you might have said no. That's why I asked. We'll get started in the morning. Good night."

CHAPTER 5
A SNOWY RIDE HOME

Friday, 26 November: *That's strange; that sounds like a rooster,* thought Audrey. She started to sit up, but her aching muscles protested. Her bed felt hard. The rooster crowed again, and she slowly opened her eyes. Strangely, she was on the floor beside a stove. It took a minute to remember what had happened the night before.

"Good morning, Miss Benton. Breakfast will be late this morning due to last night's fire. Tea, however, will be served shortly," said Brad.

"Brad," muttered Audrey, "you exasperate me sometimes. My arms ache, my back aches. How can you be so cheerful this early in the morning?"

"There's a lot to be cheerful about. We have a whole day ahead of us and no school. Plus, as you suggested last night, we can begin figuring out who set the fires."

"I did say that, didn't I?" she said, easing herself upright. "Ohhh," she groaned, "I'm sore."

"You really worked that pump last night; you ought to be sore. I'll bridle the horses for you."

"I'm always thankful when you do that," replied his sister, "but today, I'll appreciate it a lot more than usual."

"I thought you might like to freshen up before everyone else comes down. I've started the fire in the kitchen range. The Bevinses will be down in a minute, and so will Ma, Pa, and Nana.

"Thanks, Brad; I would."

The families had breakfast and talked about the fire. Immediately afterwards, Brad bridled and saddled Blaze and Ebony. Then he hitched his father's horse to the buggy.

The women hugged each other, said their good-byes, and agreed that the two families should have dinner together again, maybe in January. The men stood in the backyard and surveyed in daylight the damage caused by the fire.

"It doesn't look that bad today," said Mr. Bevins, examining the fire-blackened side of the house.

"No, it doesn't," agreed Mr. Benton. "It could have been a lot worse."

"Thank goodness the snow kept the porch floor from catching fire," said Brad.

"I never thought I'd be thankful for a snowstorm, but I am for this one," declared Mr. Bevins.

"Some scraping and painting this summer, and it will be as good as new," said Mr. Benton.

While the men discussed the fire, the women finished visiting.

"Audrey," said Wilma Sue, "that dress you're going to wear to the dance sounds delightful."

"Brad said he liked it, too," replied Audrey. "And the yellow dress you showed me is lovely. Do you think the boys will notice it?"

"Probably not," lamented Wilma Sue, "but it would be nice if they did."

"Didn't Brad promise you a dance?"

"Yes, but he'll probably forget."

"I'll remind him," said Audrey.

"Oh, no, don't do that; you might embarrass him," said Wilma Sue.

"I wouldn't do that," Audrey assured her. "I'll just quietly remind him of his promise when the time is right."

As the conversation progressed from the fire to the trip into town, the men headed toward the barn.

"I've got a small, shallow crate in the barn," said Mr. Bevins. "I'll put some burlap bags on the bottom, then the rocks that are heating on the kitchen stove. Add a few burlap bags on top, and the ladies will have warm feet for their trip home."

He walked into the barn, returning a few minutes later with the crate. "Here you go," he said, handing it to Mr. Benton.

"It feels pretty solid."

"And here's some burlap bags," he said, rummaging in an empty feed bin. "Let's add the rocks, and you can be on your way."

Mr. Benton set the crate on the kitchen floor, and Brad placed several burlap bags in the bottom. Mr. Bevins used a flat-bottomed shovel with a short handle to transfer the hot rocks from the kitchen stove to the wooden crate.

"That will keep them warm," said Brad, carefully tucking a couple of burlap bags on top of the rocks.

"Ladies, your chariot waits," announced Mr. Benton. "Brad and I are taking a foot-warming box out for you."

They carried the box of hot rocks out to the buggy and carefully placed it on the floor. Brad used a few short pieces of rope to tie the box down.

"That is going to make the trip home very comfortable indeed," said his mother as Brad helped her into the buggy.

The horses trod slowly down the glistening white road, their hooves kicking up small clouds of loose snow that the gentle breeze blew off the road. Brad and Audrey rode in front, breaking the way for the buggy.

"Brad, you didn't eat very much for breakfast," remarked Audrey, glancing at her brother. She noticed that he was beginning to look more like their father each day with his black wavy hair, posture in the saddle, and sauntering gait. His voice sounded more mature, too. Well, he was thirteen years old, only a year younger than she.

"After Thanksgiving dinner yesterday and then the fire meal last night, I wasn't that hungry this morning."

"You're quiet, too. Are you thinking about what happened?"

"Yes, I thought we might talk to Reverend Wesley and Sheriff Tate about any people new to Riverton."

Suddenly, they heard shouts coming from behind them. "Brad! Audrey! Help!" called their father.

The buggy had gone off the road and into the bar pit. Brad and Audrey turned their horses around. They clucked and firmly pressed their heels against the horses' flanks. In seconds, the horses were back at the buggy.

"Is everyone okay?" hollered Brad as he dismounted.

"Everyone is fine," his father replied. "The drifting snow hid the ditch, and the buggy slid off the road."

Audrey sidestepped Blaze until she was right beside Pa's horse, which was rather excited. "Everything's going to be all right, Ginger," she said, smoothly stroking the horse's neck. Ginger relaxed as Audrey kept a firm grasp on the bridle and continued talking soothingly to her.

Brad tied one end of a rope around his saddle horn and the other end around the front axle of the buggy. While he was tying the rope, his father helped their mother and grandmother out of the buggy.

"We're ready," said their father. "Audrey, put a rope around Ginger's neck and tie it to your saddle horn, just in case she spooks."

Audrey did as her father asked, and kept the rope short. Brad and his father went down into the ditch and started pushing the buggy.

"Back, Ebony, back," instructed Brad as they pushed.

Ebony faced the buggy and slowly backed up, just as she did when Brad tied a calf for branding. Audrey clucked and coaxed Pa's horse forward until the buggy was out of the ditch.

"Easy, girl," said Audrey, holding the horse's harness. "You're out of the ditch. As soon we get home, we'll get you settled in the barn and give you a scoop of oats."

Brad untied his rope, coiled it, and put it back on his saddle. Audrey continued to soothe Ginger while her father checked the harness and other tack for damage.

"Everything looks fine," he said. "Ladies, let's get back in so we can be on our way."

Mr. Benton climbed into the buggy and got a good grip on the reins. Audrey took care of her rope just as her brother had.

"Allow me, Madam," said Brad as he helped his grandmother into the buggy.

"Such a gentleman," she said.

"Mrs. Benton," grinned Brad, extending his arm with a flourish.

"Brad Benton," said his mother. "I don't know what I'd do without you. Thank you."

The women placed the quilt across their laps and legs and placed their feet back on the box of hot stones. Mr. Benton gently slapped the reins, and Ginger moved forward at a slow trot.

"Too many bad things have happened this Thanksgiving," commented Brad as he mounted Ebony.

"The fire last night?" replied Audrey, drawing alongside her brother.

"The Petrovs' fire, the fire last night, and now the buggy going into the bar pit," recounted Brad.

"Brad! The buggy was just an accident. The fires are what we need to worry about. One of them, and possibly both, were deliberate. We're fortunate that no one was killed or injured."

"You're right," said Brad. "The fire last night was really frightening. Let's talk to Sheriff Tate first, then Reverend Wesley."

A few minutes later, Audrey asked, "Brad, why do they call that ditch beside the road a bar pit?"

"Pa said they borrow dirt from the ditch to build up and level the road, so it's called a borrow pit, or bar pit for short. I guess they could have called it a borrow ditch or bar ditch instead."

"It's strange how words are created," said Audrey. "Miss Jones told me that the word chocolate is pronounced and spelled similarly in most languages."

Brad and Audrey chatted about the origins of words and phrases the rest of the way home. As they neared the house, Audrey suggested, "Let's ride ahead and get the fires started."

"Good idea. Pa and I got snow in our britches when we pushed the buggy. It'll be nice to be back in a warm house with dry clothes."

Blaze and Ebony were given their head, which let the horses set the pace, and they responded by breaking into a fast lope. In a few minutes, they arrived at the corral. Brad dismounted and opened the gate. The horses followed him, nickering as he opened the barn door.

"I'll leave their saddles on," said Brad. "We'll be going to town in less than an hour."

"I filled their feed boxes," said Audrey.

They entered the house, and Brad laid the fire in the kitchen range while Audrey did the same in the parlor stove. The chill was gone by the time their parents reached the house.

"My goodness," sighed their grandmother, "a warm house sure is right pleasant after that cold ride."

"Brad is upstairs changing into some dry clothes," said Audrey. "Then we're going to see Sheriff Tate."

"My Pinkertons," teased their mother. "Shall I expect you home for lunch?"

"We'll be here," replied Audrey.

It was midmorning when Brad and Audrey dismounted, looped their reins over the hitching rail, and stepped up onto the boardwalk in front of the sheriff's office. They gently stamped their feet, knocking the snow off their boots. Down the street, a couple of shopkeepers were sweeping the snow off their front steps. Water dripped from icicles on the roof of the sheriff's office, making ever-widening holes in the snow.

Brad opened the door. Sheriff Tate was at his desk, and a pot of coffee was brewing on the back of the pot-bellied stove.

"Morning, Audrey, Brad," greeted the sheriff. "What can I do for you?"

"Because of the snowstorm last night, we stayed at the Bevinses' after Thanksgiving dinner. Around midnight, someone set fire to the house," Brad informed him.

"A man threw a bottle of kerosene on the back porch," added Audrey.

"How do you know this?" inquired the sheriff, sitting up and listening attentively.

Brad and Audrey related everything that had happened. The sheriff stroked his chin thoughtfully, went to the stove, and poured himself a cup of coffee. "Do you have any ideas?"

"We're going to make a list of all the people new to Riverton since September," said Brad. "Will you help us?"

"Of course," he replied. "I must warn you. The man that set the fire last night is dangerous. Be careful who you talk to, and don't let anyone know what you're doing."

"We'll only tell you and Reverend Wesley," promised Audrey. "We'll share everything that we find with you."

"That's fair," conceded the sheriff.

For the next quarter hour, Sheriff Tate rattled off names of men and families for Audrey to write down. He told them as much as he could about the people, and when he finished, Audrey had written a full page of names.

"Thanks, Sheriff," said Audrey. "This is a good start. Now we can go see Reverend Wesley."

Brad and Audrey mounted their horses and passed the general store on their way to the reverend's home.

"Good morning, again," called Mr. Bevins as he cleared the snow from the front of his store.

"Good morning," replied Brad. "We just talked to Sheriff Tate about the fire. He said he'd see you later today."

"Thanks," replied Mr. Bevins, knocking the snow off his broom. "He usually stops by every morning."

A minute later they reached Reverend Wesley's house. Brad raised his gloved fist and knocked.

"Brad, Audrey," said Mrs. Wesley, opening the door. "Please come in. Bob is in the parlor talking with Father O'Brien. I'll tell him you're here."

"Father O'Brien?" Audrey looked at her brother quizzically.

"He's the Catholic Priest Reverend Wesley told us about last Sunday," reminded Brad.

"Audrey, Brad," greeted the reverend, coming out of the parlor. "I'd like you to meet Father O'Brien."

"Your reverend was just telling me about you two," said the priest, extending his hand.

"Welcome to Riverton," said Brad.

"Yes," added Audrey, "welcome to Riverton. Reverend Wesley told us that you were coming here to establish a Catholic Church."

"That's what my bishop wants me to do."

"What can I do for the Bentons today?" asked Reverend Wesley.

"We had Thanksgiving dinner with the Bevinses," began Brad.

"And because of the snow, we stayed overnight," continued Audrey.

"Someone set fire to their house last night. We'd like to talk to you about it," said Brad.

Brad and Audrey described the fire. Reverend Wesley asked several questions, as did Father O'Brien.

"We talked to Sheriff Tate earlier and made a list of people new to Riverton," said Audrey, handing him the list. "Do you know anyone that we should add to the list?"

Reverend Wesley studied it and said, "The Kristoffersons aren't on your list. Last month I met with them about joining the church, but they declined. Mr. Kristofferson said he was Catholic, as were his parents and grandparents. They weren't interested in coming to a Protestant church." Turning to Father O'Brien, he said, "I'll introduce you to them. They appear to be fine people, the kind that will help your new church grow."

"Fine people are needed," nodded Father O'Brien.

Reverend Wesley looked back at the list, then at

Brad and said, "I can't think of any more people new to Riverton. If I do, I'll let you know."

"Thanks," said Brad. "We'll see you tomorrow at the Petrovs' house-raising."

"You'll see me there, too," said Father O'Brien. "I've helped build several houses, and it's a good way to meet people."

"Please be careful," warned the reverend. "The man that set the fires is an arsonist. He's dangerous."

Audrey had finished setting the table and was starting to light the living room lamp when her father came in the front door.

"Audrey," he said, giving her a hug, "the *Riverton Herald* published an open letter from Reverend Wesley to the arsonist. You and Brad must read it."

Brad overheard as he entered the room with an armload of wood. He filled the wood box, picked up the newspaper, and spread it on a corner of the dining room table. Audrey hung the lamp on the wall and joined her brother to read the letter. It was in large bold type and took up half a page.

To the man who set the fires:

So far no one has been hurt by your fires. Please contact me before someone is killed or injured. You can see me after the Sunday morning church service, write me a letter, or come to my home. Our meeting will be confidential. I will not

disclose your identity to the authorities. If you set another fire, it may harm someone. Please see me before that happens. Let me help you.

Reverend Wesley

"An open letter in the newspaper to the arsonist," said Brad. "The reverend is really working to stop the fires."

"He's doing the Lord's work," said their grandmother. "The reverend is supposed to help people, just like a doctor. The doctor helps those that are injured and physically ill. The reverend treats the spiritual health of folks. The man that set the fires is spiritually ill; he needs the reverend's help."

"I hadn't thought of it that way," said Brad.

"I hadn't either," said his sister looking at their grandmother.

"Supper's ready," called Mrs. Benton from the kitchen.

In a few minutes everyone was seated, Mr. Benton said grace, and dinner was served. Brad and Audrey shared their visits to Sheriff Tate and Reverend Wesley, and their meeting Father O'Brien.

"I've been thinking about the fires," said their father. "Since the man knew Brad, it's just possible that he may set fire to our house. We need to be prepared for that."

"We can put some buckets of water and sand in the parlor," suggested Brad.

"And some old wool blankets, too," added Audrey.

"Let's make sure that the windows will open, just in case we can't get to the doors," said their father.

"We should start right after supper," said their mother. "We can't be ready too soon."

Audrey and Nana cleared the table and did the dishes. Mrs. Benton withdrew to the attic to gather some old blankets. Brad took a lantern off the kitchen wall peg, lit it, and went out to the barn with his father.

"These old buckets leak, but they'll be good for sand," said Brad. "We can get the sand from the bank of the creek."

"I'll carry the shovel and buckets," said his father. "You take the lantern."

As they waded through the snow toward the creek, the lantern cast a yellow sheen on the landscape, contrasting with the pale gray of the moonlight. Halfway to the creek, a deer darted out from a small clump of trees, splashed through the creek, and disappeared into the woods.

"Wow! I wasn't expecting that," exclaimed Brad. "My heart felt like it was going to jump out of my throat!"

"Mine, too," said his father.

"Here's the sandbank," said Brad as they approached a bend in the creek. His father shoveled away the snow and the top layer of ice-hardened sand.

"Hmm, this sand is pretty dry," said his father, dumping his shovel into a bucket. "There's a little ice in it, but we can still use it."

"I'll put the buckets on the stone pad under the stove," said Brad. "That way, any water that leaks out will go on the stones, not the wood floor."

When they had filled the buckets with sand, Brad picked up one, and his father picked up the other two and the shovel. By now the moon was higher and brighter, softly illuminating the icy countryside. The light from the windows beckoned them to come enjoy the warmth of their house. When they reached the back porch, Brad set his bucket down and held the door open for his father.

"Three buckets of sand," noted Audrey as they came into the kitchen. "I hope we don't have to use them."

"After I put these in the parlor, I'll get the buckets for the water," said Brad, hanging his lantern on one of the ceiling hooks.

"Ma's already put some old blankets in the dining room," said Audrey.

"I agree, let's just hope we don't have to use them," said their grandmother, pouring herself a cup of tea as Brad set the buckets by the stove.

He unhooked the lantern and headed to the barn, quickly returning with four buckets for the water and some checkerboard-size scrap boards.

"What are the boards for?" asked Audrey.

"To put the water buckets on," replied Brad. "Ma told me to put them on boards so the floor won't get rust circles." Brad put two water buckets against the wall by the parlor door, one next to the front door, and the last one in the kitchen. Abby had already tucked one blanket behind the wood box and another over the back of a chair at the dining room table.

"Audrey," said her father. "Please ask everyone to come here. I need to teach them how to fight a fire."

Audrey relayed her father's request, and Brad followed them into the parlor.

"We're ready, Pa," said Audrey.

"I hope the reverend's appeal is successful," began

Mr. Benton. "If it's not, we must be prepared. The sooner a fire is attacked, the better. Each second it is allowed to burn unchecked, the more likely we are to lose the house. The arsonist has used a bottle of kerosene for his past two fires; he'll probably use kerosene if he tries again."

The women nodded in agreement. Brad and Audrey looked warily at each other, and then back at their father.

"There'll probably be a fire on the floor from the kerosene. Throw a third to half a bucket of sand at a time on it. The sand will help soak up the kerosene, keep it from spreading, and slow its burning. If the sand is deep enough, it will stop the fire. Don't expect to extinguish the fire with one bucket of sand; use all the buckets. Don't worry about getting the room dirty. We can clean a dirty room - we can't clean a house that's burned down."

"What about the blankets?" asked Audrey.

"If the flames are on the walls or furniture, throw water on them. After the sand and water buckets are empty, cover any fire with a blanket. The wool won't burn easily, and we'll have time to refill the buckets with water and douse the blankets or anything else that is smoking or burning. Don't be concerned about using too much water; using too little would be worse. Any questions?"

"Do you think he'll attack our house?" asked Mrs. Benton.

"Yes, I do," said her husband. "He recognized Brad; I expect he'll try to set fire to our house."

CHAPTER 6
THE HOUSE-RAISING

Saturday morning, 27 November: Brad and his father arrived at the Petrov homestead around nine o'clock. A few other folks were already there. Mr. Bevins' wagon was by the barn with several kegs of nails, glass for windows, boxes of assorted building materials, a kitchen range, and a pot-bellied stove.

"I see ya' made it," greeted Jake Jackson. "We'll show that varmint he can't burn down a house and git away with it."

"Who else is coming?" asked Brad.

"More folks'n ya kin shake a stick at," grinned Jake. "Join the reverend; he's supervisin' the joist-layin'."

"Morning, Harold, Brad," said the reverend. "A lot of folks volunteered. We'll probably have the house up by mid-afternoon. We put the foundation blocks in last Tuesday. Some men are finishing the root cellar now. Why don't you take your shovels and join them?"

Brad and his father returned to their horses and grabbed their shovels. As they headed to the root cellar, they surveyed the men already working on the house as well as those men arriving on horseback or in wagons. Two women were circulating among the men serving coffee.

"Harold, Brad, welcome to the six-man cellar team," said Len Reno. "Angus McTavish will be arriving later with a load of stones. We'll use some of them for the steps."

"This is going to be a nice house," said Mr. Benton.

"Larger and nicer than the one that was burned," confirmed Len. "The attic will be unfinished. They might want to finish it later, maybe make it a bedroom, but that's their choice. Now, about this cellar; with an eight-man team, we'll be done in a half hour."

The eight of them dug furiously until they reached the depth and width that Jake Jackson had specified. Brad breathed heavily, leaned on his shovel, and inspected the earthen cavity he had helped create. The other men were also resting against their shovels, breathing like horses after a long run.

"That was good, men, and fast too," congratulated the reverend, peering down into the root cellar. "Put your shovels away, get a cup of coffee at the chuck wagon, and relax for a bit. We'll be laying the joists next, followed by the floor and walls."

It was now mid-morning, and about fifty men and ten women were busily working at the Petrov homestead. Some of the men could spare only a few hours, so there was a revolving group all morning.

Mrs. Petrov brought coffee to the workers and personally thanked them for coming. Mrs. Benton and other women were beginning to lay out a marvelous lunch. Sarah Davis, Doc Adams' new nurse, provided medical treatment for the inevitable cuts, splinters, and bruises.

By ten-thirty, the men had finished the floor and

were working on the walls. The two chimneys completed earlier had been built about five feet higher than the future roof. A short stovepipe protruded from the side of each chimney below where the ceiling would be. When the men broke for lunch, the wall studs were complete, and some of the roof beams were already in place.

"Ladies, gentlemen," began Reverend Wesley, "I'd like to introduce Father Trevor O'Brien. As I announced in church last Sunday, he'll be establishing a Catholic church in Riverton. I've asked him to say grace. Since many of you are not Roman Catholic, he'll say the prayer in English rather than Latin. Father."

Father O'Brien smiled at the men and women standing at both sides of the lunch table. The table was actually some long boards laid on wooden sawhorses and covered with cloth. There was a feast of bread, meat, potatoes, pies, cooked vegetables, and baked beans. As soon as Father O'Brien bowed his head, the men and women bowed theirs.

"Lord, thank you for bringing us together to help the Petrovs in their time of need..." While Father O'Brien was thanking the Lord, the familiar sound of an approaching wagon forced him to speak louder. The priest concluded, "Please bless this food and the people here before you. Amen."

As the other men began to eat lunch, Gino Donatelli, Riverton's telegraph operator, came over to Father O'Brien.

"Father," said Gino. "I've been going to Reverend Wesley's services for many years. When will you have your first service? I'd like to come because I'm Catholic."

"Next week," replied Father O'Brien. "Reverend Wesley will announce it in church tomorrow."

"My family will be there, Father," said Gino. "Is there anything I can do to help you?"

"Yes," replied Father O'Brien. "If you know of any Catholic families that haven't been coming to Reverend Wesley's services, please invite them to come."

"I'll do that, Father."

After lunch, the men went back to work. By two o'clock, the roof beams were completed, as were the walls. The men had built the outside and inside walls at the same time, leaving a dead air space between the boards to reduce heat loss in the winter. While the walls were going up, men were also nailing boards across the roof beams. As soon as the roof boards were done, tarpaper was unrolled across them and nailed down.

"This is wonderful. We'll be done by four o'clock, Trevor," Reverend Wesley remarked.

"The Lord helps people accomplish their own miracles," said the priest.

"Do you think the arsonist helped today?" asked Reverend Wesley.

"I wouldn't be surprised," replied Father O'Brien with a twinkle in his eye. "I wouldn't be surprised."

"Brad Benton!" declared Audrey firmly, her hands on her hips and her eyes flashing defiantly. "I am not riding a horse to the dance tonight. I am going in the buggy."

"I was just asking," responded Brad, shrugging as he lifted his open hands. "Anyhow, it will be easier if we all go together in the buggy."

There was a flurry of activity as the Bentons got ready for the house-raising dance. Nana put a couple of her pies in a box. Brad and his father hitched the horse to the buggy. The women helped each other get dressed for the evening's activities.

"The buggy's waiting," hollered Brad. "I put the pies in the back."

"Time's a-wasting," chided their grandmother. "I mustn't keep all those handsome men waiting for my arrival."

Brad checked the stoves to ensure that nothing was close enough to catch fire accidentally. He saw to it that the drafts were down to keep the fire low. When he finished, he closed the front door and ran to the buggy.

"I checked the stoves, Pa," he said, climbing into the driver's seat. "Everything is fine."

"A lot of folks will be there tonight," said his mother, as Brad gently slapped the reins.

"I talked to Wilma Sue this morning," said Audrey. "She helped Mrs. Petrov select a new dress for tonight's dance, and Harry Acker said the Petrovs were guests at his father's hotel tonight. His Pa wants them to look nice for the dance."

"We finished their house today," Brad informed them as he turned the buggy south onto the road to Riverton. "When Pa and I arrived this morning, the foundation was ready, and the root cellar was half done."

"There were six men digging," said his father. "Brad and I made it an eight-man team; we finished it up in a half hour. It's amazing what fifty men can accomplish in a day. Jake had all the materials in place. He had some men out earlier in the week to mortar the foundation columns and build the chimneys."

"Ahh, here's the school," said their grandmother. "I expect you're ready for dinner, Brad."

"I sure am," said Brad, stopping the buggy at the front door.

Brad and his father helped the ladies out of the buggy. Then his father escorted the women into the school while Brad parked the buggy behind the building with the other buggies and wagons. By the time he entered the school, the band was already on a raised platform decorated with pumpkins and tan bunting. Reverend Wesley and Father O'Brien stood in front of the band. Reverend Wesley's right hand was raised, signaling everyone to stop talking.

"Welcome," announced the reverend. "We did a very good thing this week; we helped a family in need by building a new home for them. Everyone contributed something and all those contributions made it possible. Beside me is Father O'Brien who will be starting a Catholic church. If you haven't already met him, please say hello this evening. Now, let us bow our heads and thank the Lord."

Heads were bowed while Reverend Wesley thanked God for bringing everyone together, for the house-raising, and for the food. He concluded his prayer with, "Lord, please help the person who started the fires. Remove his hatred and replace it with kindness. Please let us help him. Amen."

Brad immediately headed to the food, as did the other men who had worked on the house. The women chatted with each other as they served. Several families edged their way to the bandstand to talk to Father O'Brien.

"Brad, I don't know if you remember; I'm William Brock."

"Yes," said Brad, "Jake Jackson introduced us last Sunday. I also saw you at the house-raising today."

"Being new to town, a house-raising is a good way to meet people," said William.

"It sure is," agreed Brad. "Jake said over a hundred men spared some time to help build that house."

"I understand the Petrovs are Russian Jews," said William. "I wouldn't have thought so many people would help them."

"The Petrovs are good people," declared Brad. "Their religion didn't make any difference to the people helping them. We're all together in a rugged country, and we have to help each other. We can't let differences in race, religion, or the country someone came from determine whether or not we help them."

Audrey stopped to listen as her brother spoke.

"Your father seems to be in better health today than he was last week," observed William. "Was he sick?"

"He was shot and left to die by Duke Badger," stated Audrey in a subdued voice.

"What?" he sputtered, moving a bit to make room as another man joined them. "Shot and left to die? Why?"

"Duke Badger held up the stage we were on. When he discovered the strongbox was empty, he took the driver's shotgun and shot a large hole in the stage door. Then he took my father captive and shot the driver."

"Evening," said the man who had joined them.

"Bob Black's my name. About that holdup; the driver shouldn't have tried to stop it."

"He didn't," insisted Brad. "The driver didn't even have a gun when Duke shot him."

"That's right," chimed in Jim Bates, strolling over to them. "I'm the driver he shot. I would have died too, if Brad hadn't bandaged me up and driven me back to Riverton."

"Oh," said William. "I hadn't heard about that."

"Me, either," said Bob.

"Excuse me," Audrey whispered to her brother. "Wilma Sue keeps looking at you. She told me that you had promised her a dance tonight. I know you don't want to disappoint her."

"Thanks for reminding me, Audrey." Turning back to the group, he continued, "Mr. Bates and Audrey will tell you about the robbery. I'll catch up with you later."

Wilma Sue noticed Brad coming toward her, smiled, and stood up. She was wearing a form-fitting yellow dress with white lace around the neck and wrists. Her hair hung in loose curls down to her shoulders.

"Wilma Sue, that is a very nice dress."

"Thank you. This is the first time I've worn it."

The band finished playing, and the caller announced the next song. Brad turned to check out the band. There was a guitar, a banjo, a small bass drum, a snare drum, a violin, and a tuba. Swiveling his head back to Wilma Sue, he said, "Shall we dance?"

"Yes, I'd like that."

They joined one of the squares just before the caller began. There were four squares of dancers. Some of the people clapped; others just watched. When the song was over, most couples waited for the next dance, but some, like Brad and Wilma Sue, left the floor.

"Who were those men you were talking to?" she asked.

"William Brock and Bob Black," replied Brad. "We talked about the Petrovs. Then William asked about Pa's health, so I started telling them about the holdup. Audrey and Mr. Bates were finishing the story when I left."

"Would you like a piece of pie?" asked Wilma Sue.

"Yes, will you have one too?"

"I'll come with you," she said. "I'd like you to try a piece of the pumpkin pie I baked this morning."

Audrey glanced over at her brother talking with Wilma Sue and said, "I don't think Brad's coming back. He and Wilma Sue are going over to the dessert table."

"Since they're occupied, Miss Benton," said William, "would you be so kind as to be my partner for the next dance?"

"Yes," she replied. "Thank you for asking me."

As they proceeded to a square, William said, "Your description of the holdup was quite intriguing. I find it hard to believe that a robber would shoot an unarmed man."

"So did I," divulged Audrey. "I believe Duke Badger shot Mr. Bates just to be mean."

The band began playing, and Brad gazed at his sister dancing with William.

"Brad, what are you looking at?" inquired Wilma Sue.

"Audrey is dancing with William Brock. He's new to Riverton."

"He's come into the store a few times," she said. "He's very polite and speaks as if he is well-educated."

"What about Bob Black?" Brad asked.

"I've served him a number of times, too. He appears to be a nice man, despite some strange mannerisms."

"What do you mean?"

"Sheriff Tate entered the store a few times when I was getting things for Mr. Black. When he saw the sheriff, he would claim he was in hurry, pay for his items, and quickly leave. It was as if he was afraid of the sheriff."

Harry Acker approached them. "Wilma Sue, may I have the next dance?"

"Certainly," she said, taking hold of Harry's arm.

As Brad's eyes followed Harry and Wilma Sue to the dance floor, he pondered what she had said. A finger poked him in the ribs, interrupting his thoughts.

"You must be deep in thought," observed Audrey. "I said your name twice before I poked you."

"Sorry, Wilma Sue told me something, and I was contemplating what it could mean."

"What was it?"

"She said she's served Bob Black a number of times. A couple of times Sheriff Tate entered, and Mr. Black got nervous, quickly leaving the store."

"Like he was afraid of the sheriff?" asked Audrey.

"Yes."

"Well, I had a dance with William Brock," said Audrey. "He's so well-mannered and bright, too well-educated to be a stable hand at the livery. I'm flattered that he would ask me to dance."

"He wants to get to know people, he's polite, and you look very nice tonight," responded Brad.

"Maybe he was just being polite," said Audrey, blushing. "Oh well, let's just enjoy the dance tonight.

Tomorrow we can talk with Nana about what we've learned."

U

Sunday, 28 November: The morning sun beamed through the east window of the church, illuminating the golden oak cross behind the altar. Rays of sunlight reflected off the cross and the white altar cloth, bathing the church in their warmth. Reverend Wesley was finishing his sermon, and he had the congregation totally absorbed in his explanation of the Ten Commandments. Father O'Brien was alternately studying the reverend's presentation and the congregation's reaction.

"Abby," signaled the reverend.

Mrs. Benton began playing the offertory hymn, Reverend Wesley stepped down from the pulpit, and the ushers began collecting the offering. Afterwards, the reverend strode to the front of the congregation where he usually made his announcements.

"Ladies and gentlemen, fellow Christians," he began. "Thanks to all of you for helping make the Petrovs' house-raising, and the dance, a success."

There was a murmur of approval from the congregation.

Reverend Wesley continued, "Many of you met Father Trevor O'Brien yesterday. If you didn't, please say hello to him after the service. We have worked out a schedule to share the church; Father O'Brien will tell you about it."

"Thank you," said Father O'Brien. "This is a diverse country. Its citizens represent many denominations. I'm pleased to be able to share the Lord's work in Riverton with your reverend. Now, about the Catholic services, there'll be two masses each week, starting next Sunday. One will be Saturday evening at seven o'clock, and the other will be Sunday morning at half past eight. We'll determine the Christmas schedule later this week. I look forward to celebrating our first mass with those of you who are Catholic and hope you will spread the word to any who are not here with us this morning."

Father O'Brien turned and nodded to Reverend Wesley.

"Before the closing hymn, I have a special announcement," said the reverend. "This announcement is for the man who burned the Petrovs' house and set fire to the Bevinses' house. I know that you've been to some of my church services. If you're here today, please hear me. What you're doing is wrong. Please come see Father O'Brien or me. Let us help you before someone is hurt or killed by your actions. If you're setting the fires out of hate, you must stop. That hatred will grow and grow, like a weed in a garden. Hate is a horrible disease that will destroy you. The longer you wait, the worse the hate will become. Hate opens your heart to Satan. Hate will ravage your soul. Hate will make you a hollow man, hollow like a tree that has had its heart devoured by termites. You'll become a beast, a beast in the body of a man. You'll never be free from the urge to hate more, the urge to burn more. You'll never be satisfied. Please come to us. Let us help you."

Silence filled the church. No one moved or talked after; the reverend's plea resonated within each person. After a pause that seemed like an eternity, Reverend Wesley whispered, a whisper that was heard through the entire church, "Abby, the closing hymn, please."

CHAPTER 7
THE FUNERAL

Saturday, 4 December: Brad and Audrey halted their horses in front of the stage office and dismounted. The sky was a cloudless deep blue, and fresh white snow covered the trees, ground, and houses. The countryside looked as though a giant sifter of flour had passed over it during the night.

"I'll build a fire," said Brad as he unlocked the front door. "The office should be warm by the time Pa arrives."

"He always wants a cup of coffee, too," said Audrey, picking up the coffeepot.

By the time Brad had the fire going, Audrey was back with the coffeepot full of water. She had finished the dusting and Brad was sweeping the floor when they heard footsteps on the boardwalk.

"Good morning, Audrey, Brad," said Sheriff Tate as he entered. "I see you're getting the place ready for your Pa."

"It's one of our Saturday chores," replied Audrey. "Pa should be here in about ten minutes. Shall we tell him you stopped by?"

"No need to do that. My news is really for the two of you."

Brad set aside his broom and looked at the sheriff

expectantly. The slow drip of melting snow striking the boardwalk punctuated the stillness of the morning.

"There was another fire last night," the sheriff divulged. "Old Man Abbott's place."

"He lives in that small shack about a mile west of here, doesn't he?" asked Audrey.

"That's the one," said the sheriff. "It's falling apart, but it's all the old man has."

"What about Mr. Abbott?" prodded Brad.

"He wasn't there last night. He's getting along in years, and his Civil War wounds have been bothering him of late. He was feeling poorly, so when he came into town for supplies yesterday, he dropped in to see Doc Adams. The doc had just raised his stethoscope to the old man's chest when Abbott up and collapsed. Doc Adams kept him in his office overnight."

"Does Mr. Abbot know that someone burned his home?" queried Audrey.

"Not yet," said the sheriff. "He may never know, either. Doc Adams told me he doesn't have long to live; he may not even last the day. I'm going for the reverend now."

"That's a shame," Audrey remarked. "He's such a nice man."

"How old is he?" asked Brad.

"His best guess is about 55," said the sheriff. "Like so many orphans, Abbott doesn't know when or where he was born, or even who his parents were. He drove supply wagons for the Union Army during the Civil War."

"We've always known him as Old Man Abbott," said Audrey. "What's his first name?"

"Tobias," replied the sheriff.

"How did he get wounded?" asked Brad. "I thought supply wagons stayed behind the battle lines."

"Well, they usually do. In one of the battles, and don't ask me which one, the men in his unit were short on ammunition, hadn't eaten since the previous day, and were out of water. So Tobias filled his wagon with shot, powder, barrels of water, and boxes of food. Then he whipped his team of horses to a gallop in a deadly race to get to his men before the Confederates could shoot him. Well, he surprised the Confederates and managed to reach his men before the Rebs could stop him. Although he drove his wagon to a draw where he couldn't be seen, the Rebs had a pretty good idea where he was hiding. They elevated their artillery to bombard that draw. The Union soldiers predicted that the Rebs would do just that, so they unloaded that wagon faster than a frog eating a fly. The bombardment wounded some of the Union soldiers, including Tobias. The shelling angered the Union troops so much that they decided to teach Johnny Reb a lesson. In the middle of the night, some volunteers snuck behind Confederate lines and started shooting in both directions at the same time. Well, when the Rebs woke-up and started firing back, the Union boys stopped and snuck back to their lines. Having no clue that the Union boys had left, the Rebs kept shooting at each other in the dark. Meanwhile, the Union boys just hunkered down and went to sleep. First thing next morning, they charged the remaining sleepy Confederates and forced them to retreat."

"Wow, that is some story," said Brad.

"There's more," continued the sheriff. "Tobias got a

medal for his bravery. He's always been proud of that medal and considers the Army his family. He told Doc Adams, the reverend, and me that he wants to be buried in his uniform and have "Taps" played at the graveside. He asked your Pa to be one of his pallbearers."

"Well, thanks for telling us about the fire," said Brad.

Sheriff Tate looked at them and confessed, "I haven't a clue as to who is setting these fires, or why."

"We don't either," said Brad.

"Well, if you two come up with one of your plans before someone gets killed, let me know," requested the sheriff.

"We will," promised Brad.

"I'm glad you told us about Old Man Abbott and the fire," said Audrey. "We'll let you know if we discover anything. See you tomorrow at church."

Brad and Audrey watched Sheriff Tate go down the boardwalk toward the reverend's house. When he disappeared from sight, they resumed cleaning the office. They worked silently, each absorbed in thoughts about Tobias Abbott and his imminent death.

Audrey spoke first, "Brad, I'm going to miss Old Man Abbott."

"The whole town will miss him," Brad responded. "He's been in every Fourth of July parade that I can remember."

"I see I waited long enough for the office to warm up," chuckled their father from the doorway. "Is that coffee I smell? Mmm."

"Sheriff Tate stopped by, Pa," said Audrey. "Old Man Abbott's house was burned while he was at Doc Adams' office last night; he may not last the day."

"He has been looking worse lately," said their father. "Does Reverend Wesley know about him?"

"He should by now," replied Brad. "The sheriff was heading to the reverend when he left here."

"Good, I brought your nana's list, Audrey," said their father, reaching into his coat pocket.

"Thanks. We'd better go now, before the store gets crowded."

They left the stage office and walked their horses to Bevins' General Store. When they arrived, two other horses were already in front. Brad and Audrey dismounted, looped their reins over the rail, and entered the store.

"Good morning, kids," said Mr. Bevins, pushing his rolling ladder to a shelf. "Wilma Sue will be right with you."

Brad glanced around the store. "Audrey, there seem to be more goods here than there used to be."

"You're right. Wilma Sue told me they have to stock more to keep up with the demand created by the new families that have come to Riverton. Now they can also offer more variety."

"I do see more bolts of cloth than in the past," Brad noted.

"Audrey, Brad," said Wilma Sue, walking over to them. "Tell me what's new while I fill your order."

"Old Man Abbott is at Doc Adams'," said Audrey, handing her the list. "He's not expected to last the day."

"Oh. He did say he believed the end was near when he stopped in last week." A tear rolled down her face. "I knew he didn't have long to live, but it's still a shock to hear he's really dying."

Brad and Audrey recounted what Sheriff Tate had told them about the latest fire and Old Man Abbott's Civil War wounds. Wilma Sue continued her inquiries as she gathered their items.

"Here's your order," she said as she added up the prices.

Reverend Wesley quietly entered the store, looked around, and then walked up behind Brad and Audrey.

Putting his hands on Brad and Audrey's shoulders, he said, "Tobias Abbott just passed away. Brad, he asked that you and your father be two of the pallbearers. I'll announce the time of the funeral at church tomorrow morning."

"Did he find out that his house was burned?" inquired Audrey.

"No," said the reverend. "We didn't see any reason to tell him. Tobias said he was ready to go, so Doc Adams let him take as much laudanum as he wanted for the pain."

"Thanks for letting us know, Reverend," Audrey responded.

"Yes, thank you." Wilma Sue dabbed her eye with her handkerchief. "I'll tell folks about the funeral as they come in. Let us know the time of the service, and I'll post a sign in the window."

"Thanks, Wilma Sue. I'll stop by when I have more information."

"We'll see you at church tomorrow," said Brad. "Thanks for telling us about Mr. Abbott's death, Reverend."

Audrey put their order in her saddlebag and looked thoughtfully at the snow-covered mountains. "The Abbott place was the third fire, Brad."

"I know," her brother acknowledged, "but for now, we need to get home. We've got homework to do, and we might not have time to finish it tomorrow."

Sunday, 5 December: Brad and Audrey tied their horses to the church's hitching rail. Buck Hodges was already there waiting for them. Together, they walked to the church entrance.

"I see Wilma Sue is already here," said Audrey. "Let's all sneak up and say 'Good morning, Wilma Sue,' together."

"All right," chuckled Buck. "On the count of three."

They crept up the steps, and Buck whispered, "One, two, three."

"Good morning, Wilma Sue," they chimed in unison.

"Good morning to the three of you. too," she laughed. "It sure is a beautiful day."

"You can say that again," agreed Brad. "The sun is shining, and the birds are singing just like we'll be doing in a few minutes."

"I heard that Old Man Abbott died," said Buck.

"Yes," confirmed Wilma Sue, "and he asked for Brad and his Pa to be two of his pallbearers."

"Reverend Wesley stopped by the store to let us know just after Mr. Abbott passed on," said Audrey.

"I hear your Ma playing the prelude," said Buck. "We'd better get inside. I'll talk to you later, Brad."

Mrs. Benton finished the prelude and began playing the opening hymn. Reverend Wesley strode down the aisle on the first verse, singing with the power of a soloist at a tent meeting. After the scriptures were read, he began his sermon. When he finished, Reverend Wesley stepped down from the pulpit and stood beside the front row of pews to make his announcements.

"As most of you already know, Tobias Abbott passed on yesterday morning. The graveside service at the cemetery will be at 2:00 this afternoon."

Reverend Wesley paused and then continued. "He led a good life and enjoyed his final years in Riverton. We had a chance to talk just before he joined the Lord. He asked the following men to be his pallbearers: Jake Jackson, Harold Benton, and Clyde Jensen were friends and fellow soldiers. Brad Benton was also a friend, as were fellow soldiers Buck Hodges, senior, and Tom Shadden, even if they were on the wrong side in the war.

Murmuring arose from the congregation as they craned their necks to see the pallbearers. Reverend Wesley waited a moment and then raised his hand for silence.

"Tobias also requested that "Taps" be played at his funeral. Luther Herseth will do the honors, since he is in town visiting his sister. He'll be leaving tomorrow for Washington D.C. to reenlist in the United States Marinc Band."

Chatter among the parishioners rose and quickly subsided when the reverend turned toward the piano and said, "Abby, the closing hymn."

Notes rang out through the church, and soon the congregation was filing out, many telling the reverend they'd be at the funeral that afternoon.

"Reverend," asked Brad, "why is Luther Herseth going to re-join the Marine Band?

"I'll try to make a long story short," said the reverend. "Luther told me he received a telegram last week from John Philip Sousa asking him to re-join the band. Sousa was appointed leader of the Marine Band last month. When I asked him to play "Taps," Luther said he had played under Sousa's direction last year in Philadelphia's Amateur Opera Company. He believes Sousa will be an excellent leader of the Marine Band. He also mentioned that Sousa's father is a trombone player in the band."

The mid-afternoon sun beat down on the mourners gathered at the cemetery. The sky was a beautiful blue with only a few small white clouds scattered across it. Horses, buggies, and wagons were tethered beside the church and in the nearby streets.

The pallbearers lined up on each side of the wagon that held the body of Tobias Abbott. Reverend Wesley nodded, and Father O'Brien gently pulled on the casket. When the bar on the side of the casket reached the first man, he grasped it and pulled it to the pallbearer beside him. In a matter of seconds, the six pallbearers hoisted the casket and started their procession to the grave.

"Slowly, men, take your time," warned Mr. Benton. "The ground is muddy."

"Watch yourselves; there's a slippery spot just ahead," said Buckley Hodges.

The men reached the gravesite and carefully lowered the casket onto the boards that had been placed across the grave. Each man took an edge of the United States flag that draped the casket and gently stepped back to pull it taut over Tobias Abbot's casket. The forty-three stars were on the left side of the casket over Abbott's heart, the same place his medal had been pinned by General Garfield years ago during the Civil War.

Reverend Wesley looked out at the people gathered before him and began the service. "Blessed are the dead who die in the service of the Lord . . ."

Brad looked around him. He saw his mother, Audrey, and Nana standing next to the Bevinses. The reverend's words washed over Brad's numbed mind. He felt lightheaded and started to wobble.

"Don't lock your knees," whispered Mr. Hodges softly as he nudged Brad. "Bend your legs a little. That will keep the blood flowing so you won't pass out. Just relax."

Brad gently bent his knees and started feeling better. "Thanks."

Father O'Brien was standing beside a tree away from the gravesite. When the reverend stopped talking and closed his Bible, Father O'Brien removed his hat. He made a long wave to Sheriff Tate who stood at the top of a small knoll overlooking the cemetery.

The sheriff turned to command the men lined up before him. "Ready, aim, fire."

The men fired a volley and quickly levered new shells into the chambers of their rifles.

"Fire," repeated the sheriff.

Another volley tore through the silence.

"Fire," said the sheriff for the last time, and the honor guard fired the final volley. The sound of their shots echoed through the hills as Luther Herseth began playing "Taps."

Brad glanced up from the casket and saw a tear trickling down his father's cheek. To his left, Mr. Hodges also had wet eyes. Luther played hauntingly, caressing the top note of each small phrase, allowing it to hang delicately and fade away before starting the next phrase. The last note of was disappearing into the hills when Reverend Wesley nodded to Mr. Benton.

The other pallbearers began folding the flag against this poignant background of the final note of "Taps" and the pungent scent of gunpowder. Those paying their last respects to Tobias Abbott were washed with a flood of war memories as they watched the folding of the flag and smelled the gun smoke. The flag was folded lengthwise once, then twice. Tom Shadden held the end of the flag with the stars; Mr. Benton held the other end and slowly started folding the flag. In a few moments, the flag was folded into a triangle, and Harold held it, the point of the star-covered triangle pointing away from his body.

Mr. Benton walked to Sarah Davis and presented the flag to her. "Tobias asked that I personally give you this flag with the following words: 'Please accept this flag as thanks, from one orphan to another'."

"Thank you, Harold," said Sarah tearfully. "He told me Friday that he wanted me to have the flag. It's something I'll always treasure."

As the rest of the mourners gradually departed, Sheriff Tate, Luther Herseth, and the honor guard descended the knoll and headed back to their horses.

Mr. Benton turned to address the pallbearers. "Men, it's time to lower the casket."

They placed three long ropes under the casket and

then pulled them, lifting the casket off the boards. Reverend Wesley and Father O'Brien removed the boards and stood back.

"Easy now, let's take our time," said Mr. Benton as the men slowly changed their grips on the ropes. When the casket reached the bottom, the men retrieved the ropes, coiled them, and handed them to Buckley Hodges.

Father O'Brien respectfully picked up a fistful of dirt, released it over the casket, and murmured something in Latin.

Reverend Wesley did the same, saying, "Rest in peace, Tobias."

"There are six shovels behind that tree," pointed Mr. Hodges with a soft voice.

The men picked up the shovels and began filling in the grave. When they had finished, the earth was mounded over the site.

"The dirt'll settle," Jake Jackson assured them. "I'll come'n level it in the spring."

Mr. Hodges spoke again, "Let's get over to the school. The ladies have put together a nice spread for dinner. I presume Victoria brought her famous apple-blackberry pie, Harold?"

"She certainly did."

The men walked back to the church, got on their horses, and headed for the school. Some of the men rode double, as did Brad and his father. When they arrived, they dismounted, and Brad tethered Ebony. The pallbearers met on the front steps and entered together.

"Good job, men," said the reverend. "Thank you."

Mr. Bevins came over and said, "The ladies have an abundance of food waiting for you. David Acker provided two kegs of cider, and Abby has several gallons of lemonade. There's also coffee and tea."

"Come on, Brad, let's go check the vittles," said Mr. Hodges, putting his hand on Brad's shoulder. "I'm hungry."

Brad piled his plate with food and looked around the crowded room for a place to sit. Reverend Wesley waved him over.

"Thanks, Reverend." Brad set his plate on the table and took a seat.

"That was quite a rendition of 'Taps' by Luther," declared Father O'Brien.

"It was the first funeral I've been to where there were military honors," revealed Brad. "I can still hear 'Taps'; it's haunting me."

"It does that to most folks," replied Brad's father.

"Who composed it? There must be a story behind it." asked Brad.

"There is," began his father. "Brigadier General Daniel Butterfield, Union Army, considered the French "Lights Out" bugle call too formal, so he worked with his brigade bugler to simplify it. When the brigade bugler plays a call, the regimental buglers in that brigade hear and repeat it. If one or more of the regimental buglers didn't hear the right one, he might repeat the call of one of the other regiment's buglers."

"A few days after the battle of Malvern Hill in July 1862, the brigade bugler presented the general with his adaptation of the French "Tattoo." General Butterfield approved and gave the order for the new bugle call, titled "Extinguish Lights," to be used immediately. That's what we heard today."

"That's not the whole story," continued Mr. Hodges. "The Confederate Army liked it, too, and asked General Butterfield for some copies, which he provided."

"One more addition to the story," recalled Clyde Jensen. "There was a funeral for a Union cannoneer a few days later. The Union commander didn't want the Confederates to hear the rifle volleys and think the Union was attacking, so there were no rifles fired at the funeral, just "Taps" played by the bugler."

"It is a haunting melody for a funeral," remarked Tom Shadden. "It had the same effect on Confederates that it did on Union soldiers."

"'Taps' is now a tradition, and it's played at most military funerals," said Brad's father.

"It's even published in the Army's new *Infantry Tactics* book," Reverend Wesley informed them.

"Well," drawled Mr. Hodges, "it'll be dark soon. We'd best help clean up and get on home."

The men took their dishes to the two women at the washing table. Brad looked around the room until he saw his mother and grandmother. Joining them, he said, "I'll get the buggy."

"Wonderful. We'll be at the front steps by the time you're there," replied his mother.

Brad went out to get Ebony. He quickly mounted his horse and rode over to the Benton buggy. He tied Ebony to the back and drove the buggy up to the front of the school. His family was on the steps waiting for him.

"Thanks, Brad," said his father, holding the horse. "Help the ladies while I hold the reins."

Brad offered his arm to his grandmother, then his mother, and then Audrey.

"Why, Brad," simpered his sister, placing her hand on his arm. "You're such a gentleman. Thank you."

"Yes, m'lady," he teased.

Brad went to the rear of the buggy to untie Ebony as his father climbed into the driver's seat.

"All set, Pa," said Brad, mounting his horse.

Mr. Benton gently slapped the reins and turned the buggy toward home. In a few minutes, they reached the house. Brad helped the ladies down and then helped his father with the horses.

"It's been a long day, hasn't it, son?"

"Tiring, too," Brad confessed.

"Funerals are always wearing," his father responded. "We experience physical fatigue from labor and emotional fatigue from funerals. Doesn't matter what kind of fatigue you have; your body needs sleep and rest."

"Oh, I'll be ready for bed tonight," said Brad, putting a scoop of oats in each of the horses' feed boxes.

"Yes, I expect you will."

As they left the barn, they stopped to admire the majestic sunset, the Lord's "Taps" silently signaling the end of the day.

CHAPTER 8
FIRE AT THE BENTONS' HOUSE

Friday, 10 December: At eight o'clock that night, snow began to fall. An hour later, the Bentons went to bed. It was midnight when Victoria got up to make a pot of tea. Outside, the wind was picking up as the center of the storm reached Riverton. The swirling snow obscured the full moon, but there was still enough of a glow to see her way around the house.

She lifted the round lid off the kitchen range and set it on the back of the stove. She added some kindling and then some small sticks to the embers. Using a thin piece of kindling, she lit a kerosene lamp and hung it on the wall. She was reaching for the teakettle when there was a tinkle of glass, a '*whump*,' and the dancing light of flames in the parlor.

"Fire!" she screamed, rushing into the parlor. "Fire!"

The center of the room was ablaze. The red-orange flames crawled across the floor; black smoke darkened the ceiling. She picked up a bucket of sand and flung the sand onto the center of the fire.

"We're behind you, Nana," shouted Brad as he grabbed a pail of water and sloshed it on the fire.

"I'll start pumping water." Audrey took the empty bucket from her brother and rushed to the kitchen pump.

"No one's going to burn me out of this house," vowed their grandmother, throwing a blanket across a section of the fire.

"Nana," called Brad, throwing a second bucket of water on the blanket, "start the bucket brigade."

Their grandmother snatched up the empty bucket and rushed into the kitchen, colliding with her son-in-law. He picked her up, whirled around, and set her down by the kitchen pump. As he completed his turn, he grabbed the bucket of water that Audrey had just filled and headed back to the parlor.

"Here's another bucket," he yelled, throwing it on part of the blanket that was burning. "More is on the way!"

Brad poured sand onto the edge of the fire. "It's just about out, Pa," Brad said, choking on the smoke. Tears streamed from his irritated eyes down his soot-stained cheeks.

"I think you're right," his father confirmed, pouring water on another smoldering piece of blanket.

"Here's more water," offered their mother. "Let me light a lantern so we can be sure."

She lit a lantern, as did Nana. The two lanterns illuminated the parlor. Snow swirled through a jagged hole in the front window. Wet sand and a partially burned blanket covered the parlor floor in front of the stove. Smudges of black soot marred the white ceiling. The Bentons surveyed the floor, the ceiling, and the broken window with awe.

"We're lucky to be alive," sighed their father. "That fire could have killed us while we slept. We would never have woken up."

"Victoria," questioned Mrs. Benton, "what happened?"

"I woke up and added some wood to the fire to make a pot of tea. I had just hung up the lantern when I heard the tinkle of broken glass, a 'whump,' and saw the flames. That's when I shouted, 'Fire!'"

"Let's get this mess cleaned up," said Mr. Benton. "We'll need some boards from the barn to cover the window."

"I'll carry the lantern, and we can get some boxes for the sand and broken glass," said Audrey.

Out in the barn, Audrey held the lantern while Brad and her father picked out some boards and a piece of canvas to cover the broken window.

"Here are two boxes for the sand and glass," said her father, handing her the wooden crates.

They closed the barn door and started back toward the house. Their mother met them at the back door. "I lit some extra lanterns," she said.

Nana hung the wet blanket over the back-porch railing. Brad and his father nailed the boards and canvas over the broken window while Audrey and her mother shoveled wet sand and glass into the boxes. Several minutes later, they all stood in the parlor and assessed the damage from the fire.

"Coffee, tea, and pie are ready," called Nana from the kitchen door.

"It was a whiskey bottle with kerosene, wasn't it?" asked Mrs. Benton.

"Yes," replied her husband. "Just like the one at the Bevinses' house."

"Audrey, you're very quiet," observed Brad, helping

himself to another piece of apple-blackberry pie. "That usually means you're thinking."

Audrey smiled weakly as she looked at her brother and said, "All the fires have been on a Friday night, a Saturday night, or a holiday night."

"That must mean something," said Brad, "but what?"

"It might tell us that the arsonist doesn't have to work the next day," Audrey suggested.

"Then the arsonist probably doesn't work weekends," concluded their grandmother.

"You can talk to Reverend Wesley about new folks again tomorrow," their mother reminded them.

"You're right," said Brad. "And now, we need to get some sleep. But first, we'd better refill these water buckets, just in case."

The buckets were filled and placed along the wall by the one bucket that still had sand in it. The Bentons gazed upon the fire-damaged room one more time and went upstairs to bed.

CHAPTER 9
THE TRAP

Saturday, 11 December: The sun was halfway up when Brad pulled on his boots. He dressed, quietly left his room, and stopped in front of his sister's door. Knocking softly, he said, "I'll meet you in the kitchen, Audrey."

Brad entered the kitchen, gave his grandmother a big hug, and said, "Thanks for saving us last night, Nana."

"We were fortunate that I got up to make that pot of tea."

"We certainly were," agreed Mrs. Benton as she and Audrey entered the kitchen. "Maybe you should get up every night and make yourself a pot of tea."

"Hopefully you won't have to," said Audrey.

"You said you had some ideas last night," prodded Brad.

"I do," she replied. "We can talk about them during breakfast."

Their mother made pancakes and bacon, Brad got the fire in the parlor stove started, and Audrey set the table. The women were putting breakfast on the table when Harold Benton came down the stairs.

"You've got a shaving cut on your chin," chided his wife, kissing his cheek.

"One of the hazards of manhood and the straight-edge razor." Her husband grinned as he sat down.

Audrey poured her father a cup of coffee and took her seat.

"Harold," nodded Abby Benton.

Everyone bowed their heads while Mr. Benton said grace. Few words were spoken as the pancakes, eggs, and bacon were passed around the table. After a minute, their mother broke the silence.

"Audrey, what are your ideas about the arsonist?" she asked.

"First, the fires have been on a weekend or holiday night," recounted Audrey. "Second, it was snowing at the time of each fire. Third, the arsonist knows Brad."

"And fourth," added Brad, "he starts the fires late at night, after everyone has gone to bed."

"And fifth," Audrey continued, "he's thrown a whiskey bottle of kerosene with a cloth wick to start them."

"His victims are active in the church," said Brad, "except for the Petrovs."

"What men are new to Riverton?" asked their grandmother.

"Vasya Petrov, Father O'Brien, William Brock, and Bob Black," Audrey ticked off on her fingers.

"The Dolinskis and the Kristoffersons are new," said Brad.

"There are the Andersons and the Andersens, too," added their mother.

"And Harry Dengler," said their father. "He arrived in town about a week before the Petrovs' fire."

"I've got to write this down," Audrey decided. "There'll

be people to add to the list we made with Sheriff Tate last week."

"That's the way to think," encouraged their grandmother.

"He sets the fires during snowstorms so the snow will hide his tracks," surmised Brad.

"And he throws a bottle of kerosene so he can stay on his horse," Audrey figured. "Kerosene starts a big fire, fast, that's hard to put out."

"It's time to learn something about these new folks," Brad advised. "Let's go talk to Reverend Wesley, Sheriff Tate, and Mr. Acker. We might discover something."

Brad and Audrey donned their hats and coats, went out the door, and headed to the corral. He saddled the horses while Audrey put on their bridles. When Brad opened the gate, his sister rode out of the corral holding the reins to his horse.

"Want to race to the road?" she goaded as Brad mounted Ebony.

"The way Ebony is bobbing her head; I know she wants to."

"On three: One, two, three!"

The horses bolted forward; Ebony started ahead by a neck, but by the time they reached the road the horses were even. Once on the road to Riverton, the horses slowed to a comfortable trot. Ebony snorted and Blaze gave a soft nicker as they matched gaits side by side.

A few minutes later they came into Riverton and turned down the street where the reverend lived. Brad and Audrey stopped their horses in front of the Wesley house, dismounted, and looped their reins over the hitching rail. Blaze and Ebony snorted and pawed the ground after their morning ride, their breath producing small clouds of steam in the chilly morning air.

"Catching the arsonist is going to be a lot trickier than finding the Big Foot Gang," said Brad, knocking on the reverend's door.

Memories of the Big Foot Gang raced through Brad's mind. He recalled that last fall, when he, his sister, and their friend Running Bear discovered the hideout of a gang that had robbed the stage. In the process of capturing the gang, Brad and Running Bear tricked them into believing that they were all captives of Big Foot. Running Bear convinced the outlaws that since he was an Indian, he could talk to Big Foot. So, in return for the gold from the stage robbery, they thought Running Bear rescued them from Big Foot. In actuality, they became prisoners of Sheriff Tate.

"It's also going to require some evidence," added Audrey. "All we have right now are some guesses, and we could be completely wrong."

"Good morning," said Mrs. Wesley. "Please come in; Bob has just finished his breakfast."

Brad and Audrey entered and waited while Mrs. Wesley fetched her husband.

"Hello you two," greeted the reverend. "Let's go into the parlor."

They entered the room, and he motioned for them to have a seat. He set his cup of coffee on a small oak table and slowly lowered himself into his stuffed leather chair.

"What can I do for you this morning?" he asked.

"We'd like to talk about the four fires," said Brad.

"Four?" said the reverend. "Don't you mean three - the Petrovs', the Bevinses', and Abbott's houses?"

"No, four fires," Brad replied. "He set fire to our house last night."

"That's terrible," said the reverend, leaning forward in his chair. "How bad was it? Is everyone all right?"

"We're fine. There's smoke on the parlor ceiling, the rug was burned, and the floor is scarred," Audrey recounted.

"Nana was up making herself some tea when the arsonist threw a bottle of kerosene through the front window," said Brad. "She yelled 'Fire,' threw a bucket of sand on it, and then a bucket of water."

"Her prompt action saved us," declared Audrey. "A blanket, more water, and another bucket of sand extinguished the fire."

"If Nana hadn't been awake when he threw the bottle, we might not have escaped," insisted Brad.

"Thank goodness we had buckets of sand and water ready in the parlor," said Audrey.

"And blankets, too; we used two buckets of sand, one of the blankets, and I didn't count how many buckets of water."

"Your preparation wasn't for naught," the reverend assured them. "It pays to be prepared."

"We've got some ideas about the arsonist," said Brad. "We'd like to share them with you and Sheriff Tate."

"This is a list of facts about the fires." Audrey handed the sheet of paper to the reverend.

Reverend Wesley read the list. When he finished, he cocked his head, pursed his lips, and looked quizzically at Brad and Audrey for a moment. Then his gaze returned to the list.

"We also made a list of Riverton's newcomers," said Brad, and Audrey gave the second sheet to the reverend.

He studied the second list for a few minutes, looked up at Audrey, and said, "It looks complete to me; however, David Acker may be able to add some names to it."

Audrey stood up, went over to the reverend, and pointed to a name on the list. "I suspect this man is the arsonist, but there's no evidence to support my belief, so it would be wrong for me to share my suspicions with anyone but you."

"You are correct about the lack of evidence," replied the reverend. "And, as you said, don't tell anyone about your suspicions. Show these lists to Sheriff Tate and David Acker. They're among the first to know about newcomers. Then I'd like you to come back to me. We need to stop these fires before someone is seriously hurt or killed."

"Thanks, Reverend," said Brad as he stood up and went to the front door. "We'll check with Sheriff Tate first."

Brad and Audrey walked down the steps to their horses. They had just unlooped the reins when they heard the front door open again. They turned and saw Reverend Wesley coming toward them.

"I almost forgot," called the reverend, "You should also talk to Mark Bevins. Newcomers always need something from his general store."

"Good idea, Reverend," said Audrey. "We'll do that."

They turned their horses toward the main street.

Brad gave a cluck and Ebony started at a fast walk; Blaze instinctively matched her pace and fell in on Ebony's right.

"So," inquired Brad. "Who is your suspect?"

"I can't tell you," Audrey replied. "You heard the reverend. I shouldn't tell anyone but him."

"But I'm your brother," argued Brad. "We're both in this together."

"True, but I might prejudice your opinion of the man. Besides, I may be wrong. Do you suspect anyone?"

"Well, yes I do."

"Why haven't you told me?" sputtered Audrey, a mischievous gleam in her eye.

Brad looked over at his sister, thought a moment, and replied with a grin, "For the same reason you didn't tell me whom you suspected. I could be wrong."

They both laughed as they dismounted in front of the sheriff's office. Stepping up to the boardwalk, they gently knocked the snow off their boots and entered the sheriff's office.

Brad opened the door, and the room's warmth enveloped them. Sheriff Tate was sitting at his desk reading the newspaper.

"Morning, Sheriff," said Brad.

"Morning, kids," replied the sheriff. "Your father told me about the fire last night; said you'd be stopping by. What can I do for you?"

"We updated the list of newcomers to Riverton," said Audrey handing it to the sheriff. "Is there anyone we should add?"

Sheriff Tate perused the list, handed it back to

Audrey, and said, "There's a new hand at the Bar-X. I believe Sam said his name is Dutch."

Audrey smoothed the sheet of paper on the desk, bent over and wrote Dutch at the bottom of the list followed by "Bar-X."

"Thanks, Sheriff. We're going to see Mr. Acker next. He might know of someone else to add to the list," reasoned Brad.

They left the sheriff's office and looked down the street. "It's so pretty," remarked Audrey. "The fresh snow covered everything last night."

"Let's walk over to the hotel," said Brad. "We can talk on the way."

"The new Bar-X hand can probably be scratched off the list," concluded Audrey as they walked down the boardwalk.

"Right," agreed Brad. "The hours they work out there eliminate them from any day except possibly Saturday night."

"We need to include everyone for now though, so I'll leave his name on the list," said Audrey.

"If we review all the names and facts, we might see something suspicious," suggested Brad."

"Here we are," announced Audrey, looking through the hotel lobby's window on her right.

Brad and Audrey walked into the Riverton Hotel and went to the door marked PRIVATE. Brad knocked twice and glanced at his sister as they waited for a response.

"Who is it?" called Mr. Acker.

"Brad and Audrey Benton," Brad responded.

"Come on in."

Brad opened the door. David Acker was seated at his large mahogany desk, a catalogue in his hand.

"Morning," said Brad.

"Good morning to you, too; what are Riverton's two Pinkertons up to today?"

"Mr. Acker," said Audrey, blushing, "Why do you think we're up to something?"

"So, you're not up to something?" Mr. Acker questioned, his eyes twinkling. "Then what brings you to my hotel so early in the morning?"

"We've made a list of newcomers to Riverton," Brad informed him. "Since you meet or know most of Riverton's residents and visitors, we'd like you to check the list. We don't want to miss anyone."

Audrey handed the list to Mr. Acker, who studied it for a minute. He peered over the top of his glasses at Audrey and said, "I have no names to add. It looks complete, but, Miss Benton, do you still say you're not up to something? It looks to me like you're searching for an arsonist. Am I correct?"

"Yes," uttered Audrey, her face flushing again.

"You're going about it the right way," Mr. Acker declared leaning back in his chair. "Make a list. Put all the names, places, dates, times, and other facts down on paper. Examine your notes carefully. Then, if you are clever, you may be able to see a pattern. But with only three fires, a pattern may be hard to find."

"Make that four fires," amended Brad. "Our house was set on fire last night."

"Your house?" Mr. Acker bolted upright, his eyes wide open in shock.

"That's right," said Audrey, her composure regained.

"Right around midnight; fortunately, Nana was in the kitchen when the bottle of kerosene was thrown through the window. She yelled 'Fire' and threw a bucket of sand on it."

"How bad was the damage?"

"Smoke on the ceiling, the carpet and a blanket burned, and the floor was scarred," replied Brad.

"When you've completed your list, be sure to share it with Reverend Wesley and Father O'Brien," advised Mr. Acker. "They're both intelligent men. They know how evil can turn good men bad. And," he paused, "they both know how to return evil men back to the path of good. Reverend Wesley will readily affirm that Father O'Brien can deflect men away from evil's path. And, if you ask Father O'Brien, he'd say the same about Reverend Wesley. With the two of them working on an evil man, I expect they'll succeed."

"I hope so," professed Audrey.

"We're going to meet with Reverend Wesley again later this morning," said Brad.

"If I hear of any other newcomers, I'll tell your father," promised Mr. Acker.

Brad and Audrey left the hotel and headed for the general store. There were two horses and a wagon tethered in front. Sam Burns and Dooley were loading supplies into the back of the wagon.

"Morning," said Brad.

"How's your Pa?" asked Dooley. "I haven't seen him for several weeks.

"Pretty good," replied Audrey. "He's just about recovered."

"Give him our best," said Mr. Burns. "Things have

been hectic, what with the snow and all. Dooley and I should be able to get to church tomorrow; if so, I'll see him then."

"All right; maybe we'll see you there. Bye, now," hollered Dooley as he slapped the reins on his two-horse team.

Brad and Audrey entered the store, stopping for a moment to let their eyes adjust from the bright sunlight reflecting off the snow before going to the counter where Wilma Sue was standing.

"Hi," said Wilma Sue. "I see you have your shopping list. I'll start filling it."

"Thanks," said Audrey, handing her Nana's list.

"I'll ask her ma about the newcomers," murmured Brad as he climbed the stairs to the store's office.

"Brad Benton," smiled Mrs. Bevins. "What brings you up here?"

"We're making a list of newcomers," said Brad handing her the list. "Could you to look at it and see if we missed anyone?"

Mrs. Bevins read down the list and said, "No, I think you've got everyone. I keep the accounts, so Mark tells me all about the newcomers."

"Thanks, Mrs. Bevins," Brad replied. "I'll see you tomorrow."

Brad went back down stairs to join his sister. Wilma Sue was totaling their order, and Audrey was putting the items into a bag when he reached the counter.

"You'll be paying cash, as usual?" assumed Wilma Sue.

"Oh, yes," Audrey handed her a half-eagle.

Wilma Sue set the five-dollar gold coin on top of the

cash drawer, counted out the change, and handed it to Audrey.

"I'll see you tomorrow," she called as Brad and Audrey walked to the door.

As soon as they left the store, Brad put a hand on Audrey's arm. She looked at him expectantly.

"Let's see Pa before we go back to the reverend."

Harold Benton sat writing a letter at his desk in the stagecoach office. *Time to add a piece of wood to the fire,* he thought to himself. As he closed the lid to the pot-bellied stove, he heard the door open behind him and spun around.

"Morning, Pa," said his children in unison.

"Good morning again," greeted their father. "Any new additions to your newcomers' list?

"Just one," said Audrey handing the list to her father. "We'd like you to check the list, too.

Harold looked at the list, glanced out the window a moment, and passed the list back to his daughter. "Can't think of a soul to add," he remarked. "What did Reverend Wesley have to say?"

"He asked us to come see him after we talked to Sheriff Tate, Mr. Bevins, and Mr. Acker," said Brad.

"Well, mustn't keep the reverend waiting," admonished their father.

"We won't," Brad assured him as he opened the door.

"We'll see you tonight, Pa," said Audrey as they left the office.

Brad and Audrey mounted their horses and headed back toward the reverend's home. The sun was melting the snow, and the ruts created by the wagon wheels were a slush of snow and mud. The horses walked down Main Street and then down the street to the reverend's house, stopping in front of it. Brad and Audrey dismounted and went to the front porch.

"Welcome back," said the reverend, opening the door. "I saw you ride up. Thought I'd save your knuckles, Brad. Come right in."

"Thanks, Reverend," he said. "Audrey and I have a plan that we'd like to share with you."

Brad and Audrey explained their idea to Reverend Wesley. When they finished, he leaned back in his chair and looked thoughtfully out the window. Audrey and Brad eyed each other hopefully, then the reverend, and then followed his gaze out the window. The dripping of icicles outside and the crackling of the fire in the stove seemed to mimic the conflicting aspects of their plan. Reverend Wesley stood up and slowly walked to the window, his hands clasped behind his back.

"It's got risks, but it's a good strategy," he declared. "If I had a better one, I'd tell you, but I don't. We need to have a meeting." He paused, pulled out his pocket watch to check the time, and continued. "Three o'clock should work. On your way home for lunch, please tell Sheriff Tate that I'd like him to come here for a meeting at three. Then to the Riverton Hotel, and tell Father O'Brien the same thing. If they ask what the meeting is about, say I have a problem that needs their help."

"Yes, sir," said Brad.

Brad and Audrey mounted their horses and headed to the sheriff's office. The temperature had climbed markedly while they were in the reverend's house; the streets were a mess of mud and melting snow. They dismounted, looped their reins on the hitching rail and stepped up to the boardwalk.

"I know Sheriff Tate is going to ask what the meeting is about," worried Audrey.

"Of course, he will. Just tell him what the reverend said."

"But he's going to want more information."

"Maybe so, we'll soon find out," said Brad, opening the door to the sheriff's office.

"Back so soon?" asked Sheriff Tate.

"Just delivering a message from the reverend," said Audrey. "He'd like you to come to a meeting at his house this afternoon at three o'clock."

"What's the meeting about?" asked the sheriff.

"He said he has a problem that needs your help," she replied.

"We're supposed to give Father O'Brien the same message," Brad added, opening the door to leave.

"Bye, Sheriff" said Audrey as the door closed.

"If we walk to the hotel," said Brad, "we can ride home with Pa for lunch."

They entered the Riverton hotel. A sign on the counter read, FATHER O'BRIEN, ROOM 201.

"That sign is new," said Brad. "I guess he wants to make sure the arsonist can come to him for help."

"Well, now we know his room number," said Audrey as they started up the stairs.

Brad raised his hand and knocked on the door. They heard the creak of floorboards as the priest crossed the room.

"Brad, Audrey," said Father O'Brien opening the

door. "I was just going down for lunch. How can I help you?"

"Reverend Wesley would like you to come to a meeting at his house at three o'clock this afternoon," related Audrey.

"I'll be there," the priest assured them. "I presume you'll be there too."

"We certainly will," confirmed Brad as the three of them reached the top of the stairs.

"Where are you going now?" asked Father O'Brien.

"To the stage office for Pa, then home for lunch," replied Audrey.

"Have a good lunch," said the priest. "I'll see you at three."

At three o'clock, Brad and Audrey dismounted in front of the reverend's house and looped their reins over the hitching rail. The singing of the chickadees and the occasional plop from a clump of slushy snow falling from a tree punctuated the silence. They paused on the way to the front door to watch a Lewis Woodpecker as it pecked on a tree, its greenish head glinting in the sunlight. The bird's staccato drumming suddenly stopped as the bird dug out devoured some unfortunate insect.

Brad knocked on the reverend's door, stepped back, and waited. Through the window, he saw Mrs. Wesley coming to greet them.

"The third time is the charm," she smiled. "Father O'Brien and Bob are in the parlor waiting for you."

Father O'Brien stood up when Brad and Audrey

entered. "Hello there. Your reverend tells me you have a plan. When the sheriff arrives, I'm looking forward to hearing it."

"Good news," answered the reverend, "he just arrived."

"Let's sit down in the kitchen," he suggested. "There's room at the table for all of us, and Martha just baked an applesauce cake that I can't wait to try."

When they were seated, Audrey set down her paper with all of the facts and the list of newcomers. The sheriff picked up the fact sheet as Mrs. Wesley served the cake.

"I have tea and coffee," offered Mrs. Wesley.

"Coffee, please," said the sheriff.

"Tea, anyone?" said Audrey picking up the teapot.

"Yes, please," said Father O'Brien.

As soon as everyone was served, the reverend bowed his head and said grace. The sheriff contemplated the lists and sipped some of his coffee while everyone else devoured the cake.

Audrey looked up at the sheriff and started laying out the plan. "If I've come to the right conclusion, the next fire will be on a Friday or Saturday night when it snows. This time of year, we shouldn't have to wait long for another snowfall."

"We believe the next families targeted will be the McTavishes, the Donatellis, and the Dolinskis," Brad informed them. "We'll need a team leader for each house that the families, and the citizens of Riverton, will trust."

"I think the three of us can fill those roles," said Reverend Wesley, eyeing Sheriff Tate and Father O'Brien. "I know some others that could also lead a team, but we're here developing the plan. Each leader should select a fire-fighting team and some lookouts. Additionally, we need men who are good riders and ropers with fast horses at each house. I'd like to capture this arsonist."

"Our two suspects' names are at the top of the list," Brad pointed out. "We have no evidence, just suspicions and coincidences. Since we may be wrong, we don't want anyone to know whom we suspect."

Audrey continued, "The next Friday or Saturday evening that it snows, each team should meet at their assigned house around nine o'clock. Brad and I will watch the suspects. If one of them leaves, we'll ring the church bell."

"Good thinking. That bell can be heard halfway to the Bar-X," remarked Sheriff Tate. "It will alert the teams that the arsonist might set another fire. It's a long shot, but it just might work."

"The other alternative is to just let the arsonist keep setting fires," observed Father O'Brien, "but if we don't take the initiative, all of Riverton could eventually be nothing more than a pile of ashes."

Sheriff Tate stood up and poured himself another cup of coffee. "As Sheriff, it's my responsibility to provide some legal guidance. There's is nothing wrong with a man riding out to someone's home at night, even if it is snowing. We must wait to act until he does something or is obviously about to do something," he advised. "We must not harm an innocent man."

"That's right. The United States was founded on the principle of justice for all, not just some," affirmed Reverend Wesley. "A man is innocent until a jury of his peers finds him guilty. The government doesn't have the right to assault a man just because someone believes he might commit a crime."

"Every man has the right to defend himself and his family," continued the sheriff. "A stranger on horseback, outside a house, lighting a bottle with a wick in it is a real threat to the family inside the house. That's sufficient justification for the homeowner to shoot the stranger. The homeowner doesn't even have to wait for the stranger to throw the bottle before shooting. The next step in the plan is to designate men for the teams.

"Buckley Hodges is a good man," suggested the reverend.

"Harold Benton can work with you at the Donatellis', Father," determined the sheriff. "I'll also request help from some of the Bar-X men tomorrow."

Brad and Audrey said they'd ask Buck Hodges, Jr. and Wilma Sue to help them watch the suspects the next time it snowed.

"I think we're ready," concluded Reverend Wesley. "I'll tell the congregation tomorrow that we need to test the rope for the church bell and that Brad will do it. Since he'll have to test it, they can expect to hear the bell on a Friday or Saturday night. I trust the Lord would approve of my lying, considering the circumstances."

"Consider it just a little fib," said the priest. "I'm sure he would approve."

Before we leave," said Reverend Wesley, "let us close with a prayer. We can certainly use God's help."

"Lord, please guide us in our effort to stop these fires. Help us show the arsonist your path..."

The reverend finished and took a bite of his cake.

"Excellent cake, Martha," complimented Father O'Brien.

"That it is," agreed the sheriff.

"Would you like another piece, Brad?" asked Mrs. Wesley.

"Yes, ma'am, it's delicious."

After a few more cups of coffee and tea with pleasant conversation, the group adjourned.

Brad and Audrey mounted their horses and turned toward Main Street. When they reached the edge of Riverton, the horses broke into a slow trot.

"Now we just have to wait for the next snow," Brad sighed.

"I hope we can stop the arsonist from burning another house," said Audrey.

"We will, if our plan works. We'll know soon enough."

CHAPTER 10
WATCHING THE SUSPECTS

Friday, 17 December: Brad and Audrey walked down the front steps of the school and started home. Brad glanced up at the dull sky and smelled the air.

"It's going to snow tonight," he announced.

"I think you're right," said Audrey. "We'd better hurry home and get ready. If it does, it's going to be a late night for us."

Brad looked to the west as they walked home. "The western sky is gray, not black, with just a gentle breeze. It won't be a blizzard, but there'll be snow."

They walked down the rutted lane to their house. It looked warm and inviting as smoke wisped up from the kitchen chimney.

"Let's feed and saddle the horses before we go in," suggested Audrey. "Then we can leave right after supper."

They entered the barn through the tack room door. Blaze and Ebony, sensing the excitement, came in from the corral and nickered. Brad rubbed Ebony's neck, went to up to the hayloft, and tossed down several forks of hay. When he finished, he climbed down to the floor of the barn.

"Don't worry, I'll give you some." Brad picked up the

pitchfork and Ebony nudged him as he tossed some hay into her stall.

"They know something is up," said Audrey, scooping some oats into the feed boxes. "Blaze is pawing the ground."

"We're lucky to have smart horses," said Brad as he laid a saddle blanket on Ebony's back.

"Maybe they're just keyed up because they haven't been ridden all week," Audrey commented.

Brad saddled both horses and tightened their cinches while Audrey put on their bridles.

"We're getting pretty good at this," remarked Brad. "We'll be ready to go right after dinner if it snows."

"Brad," said Audrey solemnly as she put her hand on her brother's arm, "I want to be wrong. I don't want either of our suspects to be the arsonist."

"I feel the same way," admitted Brad, "but we have to stop the fires. We have to find out who the arsonist is, or someone is going to die."

They closed the barn door and went to the house. Nana was stirring a large pot when Brad opened the kitchen door. The delightful aroma of stew and fresh biscuits made his stomach growl.

"All afternoon it's looked like snow," said their grandmother, "so I made venison stew and biscuits for supper. That should stick to your ribs while the two of you are out tonight. I even made extra biscuits so you could take some with you."

"Thanks, Nana," Brad gave his grandmother a quick hug. "We've saddled the horses, so we can leave right after supper."

"Your parents will be home any time now. The wood

box is getting low. If you bring in a couple of armloads before you leave, I'll keep the kitchen stove going and wait up for you tonight. A cup of tea and some oatmeal cookies will be just the thing to warm you up after chasing arsonists in the snow."

"I'll go get the wood now," replied Brad with a big smile on his face.

"I'll wash up and set the table," said his sister.

The table was set and the woodboxes filled before their parents got home. After supper, they excused themselves and went upstairs to bundle up for a cold evening. They each put on long underwear and an extra pair of socks. Audrey donned an old wool sweater that Brad had outgrown, then her scarf, coat, and hat. Brad, too, dressed warmly for the coming night and then went downstairs to the kitchen.

"Well," declared their mother, looking at them with her hands on her hips, "you two should stay warm tonight."

"We're going to stop by Reverend Wesley's first," said Audrey. "Buck Hodges and Wilma Sue are going to meet us there."

"I'll be leaving in a little bit to go to the Donatellis," their father informed them. "Reverend Wesley is the team leader for their house; I'm his backup."

"I want all three of you to come over here," said their grandmother. "Right now; give me a hug."

Harold Benton put his arm around his mother-in-law, gave her a hug, and a kiss on the cheek. "Don't worry," he said. "We're well-prepared to put out any fire and catch the arsonist."

Brad put his arm around her just like his father had

done and gave her a squeeze. "Audrey and I are just going to watch the suspects and ring the church bell if they leave."

"I'll take care of my younger brother," Audrey assured her grandmother as she gave her a big hug. "We really won't be in any danger."

"I'm so pleased that you three gave your grandmother a hug, but you better not forget me, if you know what's good for you," admonished their mother.

Mrs. Benton received her hugs, and then Brad, Audrey, and their father headed out to the barn. Blaze and Ebony came to the gate, followed by Ginger. The three of them mounted their horses and headed off toward Riverton.

As they entered town, their father said, "Tell Reverend Wesley that I'm on my way to the Donatellis."

"Yes, Pa."

Brad and Audrey turned down the street to the Wesley's' home. They passed several houses, some illuminated by lanterns that had been lit for the evening. In a few of the houses, the flickering fireplaces were visible through the windows.

They stopped their horses, dismounted, and walked up to the reverend's front door; Brad knocked and said, "It looks like it's going to snow gently all night."

"I see you're ready for a long, cold night," said Mrs. Wesley as she held the door open for them.

"Yes, ma'am," replied Brad.

"Fortunately, it's not a blizzard," added Audrey, unbuttoning her coat.

"Buck and Wilma Sue are already here," said Mrs. Wesley. "They're in the kitchen with Bob."

"Brad, Audrey," greeted Reverend Wesley. "I'm glad you're here. I'm getting ready to leave for the Donatellis' house."

"Pa asked us to tell you that he's on his way there now," said Brad.

"Good. Buck and Wilma Sue will watch the first suspect. Brad, you and your sister can watch the second. Don't take any chances. You can keep an eye on each other while you're on duty."

"We're ready," declared Buck, helping Wilma Sue with her coat.

Brad opened the front door and ushered everyone out. The reverend mounted his horse, pulled his hat low, and departed for the Donatellis'.

"Pa gave me a key to the stage office," Audrey informed the others. "He told me that if the weather gets bad, we should stay there overnight."

Buck stopped in front of the hitching rail. "Let's review the code. One wave of my hat means the suspect headed north. Two waves of my hat means he headed south, and three means he headed east. We pause and then repeat the code."

"Right," said Brad.

Buck helped Wilma Sue onto his horse first. Once mounted, Wilma Sue took her foot out of the stirrup so Buck could mount. When Buck was seated behind the saddle, they left the reverend's house. The three horses rode abreast, turned the corner, and headed down Main Street.

"We can hitch our horses in front of the sheriff's office," Brad advised. "That's halfway between the two suspects."

A few minutes later, they stopped, dismounted, and tied the reins to the sheriff's hitching rail. They stepped up onto the boardwalk and looked up and down Riverton's Main Street.

"We'll open the window and wave to you when we're ready," said Buck.

"We'll do the same," replied Brad as he and Audrey headed to the stage office.

Audrey unlocked the front door. Once inside, Brad closed the door, and his sister locked it. They stood still for several minutes, letting their eyes adjust to the darkness.

"There's the opening to the attic." Audrey moved toward the ladder on the wall.

"I'll go first," said Brad. "I'll pull you up the last few feet."

Brad quickly climbed up the ladder nailed to the wall, pushed back the trap door, and pulled himself into the attic. When Audrey was at the top rung of the ladder, Brad reached down for her. They grasped each other's wrists, and with his feet astride the opening, Brad bent over and pulled her into the attic.

"Thanks, I'd never make it up here without your help."

"Let's move over to the window," suggested Brad. "From there, we can see our suspect and Buck, too."

Audrey settled down on a packing crate and looked down the street to see Wilma Sue helping Buck open the attic window above the barbershop.

"I'm so glad Reverend Wesley talked to Mr. Acker about our plan," she said.

"I know," agreed Brad. "Thank goodness Mr. Acker gave him the keys to the room above the barber shop.

Wilma Sue said a man wanted to rent the room, but Mr. Acker turned him down. Told him he'd let him know when it was available. He kept the room vacant just so Buck and Wilma Sue could use it to watch their suspect."

Brad and Audrey sat on the packing crates and watched the entrance to the boarding house. Above the barbershop, Buck and Wilma Sue viewed their suspect's door

Several hours passed by with no activity from the suspects. Brad and Audrey talked about school, the fire at their house, and the Thanksgiving Day fire at the Bevinses' house.

"It must be about ten o'clock," noted Audrey. "The lamps in the hotel dining room are being extinguished."

"Look!" Brad gasped. "Our wait may be over. "Buck just gave me three waves of his hat. Now he's pausing, there's one, two, three."

"His suspect must be heading east," replied Audrey excitedly.

"And it's still snowing," grinned Brad. "Let's go ring the church bell."

They raced over to the trap door and Audrey started down the opening. Brad grasped his sister's wrists and lowered her until her foot reached the top rung of the ladder. She climbed down quickly followed by her brother. He stopped halfway down, closed the trap door, and then jumped to the floor.

"Don't open the door until we're sure no one is on the street," cautioned Brad.

"I won't," she said. "Check the south window. I don't see or hear anyone to the north."

"It's clear," announced Brad, looking out the south window. "Quick, let's go."

Audrey unlocked the door, slowly opened it, and carefully looked up and down the street once more. They exited, keeping close to the outside wall of the stage office. Audrey closed the door and locked it.

"Let's get our horses and head to the church," said Brad as they hustled to the sheriff's office. "Buck and Wilma Sue will be right behind us."

The streets were deserted, and the town was very quiet except for the noise from the saloons. When they reached their horses, Brad and Audrey mounted and headed to the church. The muddy ruts made by the wagons earlier that day were now covered with freshly fallen snow.

"Well, the first stage of the plan worked," observed Audrey. "We saw a suspect leave town when it was snowing."

"Now for the second part," added Brad, "signaling the three teams."

"Here we are," she said, stopping Blaze at one of the church's hitching rails.

They dismounted, looped their reins over the rail, and went to the side door. Brad opened it, stepped inside the church, and lit a lantern.

"I can hear a horse coming now," Audrey said. "It must be Buck and Wilma Sue."

"I think it is. I see two people on the horse."

Buck and Wilma Sue arrived and joined them.

"It sure is difficult to not call the suspects by their names," complained Buck.

"I know," replied Audrey. "But Reverend Wesley insisted that we always refer to them as suspects."

"It's better than saying a man's name and then finding out later that he was innocent," remarked Wilma Sue.

"I know," agreed Brad. "We'd feel terrible. We wouldn't want to falsely accuse a man of being an arsonist. We'd best go ring the bell. Your suspect headed east, didn't he?"

"We watched him head south, and then turn east," confirmed Wilma Sue.

"So we ring the bell three times, wait awhile, and then give it three more rings," said Brad.

"Then we wait several minutes and do it again," Audrey added.

Brad and Buck tugged the bell rope once and heard the familiar dong. They pulled two more times and stopped. A minute later, they repeated the process.

"Now we wait awhile and then do the three rings again," said Buck.

At the Donatellis' house, Reverend Wesley had his team ready. Two men from the Bar-X had their horses in the barn, saddled, and ready to ride. Harold Benton had placed buckets of sand, some blankets, and buckets of water in the kitchen and living room of the Donatellis' house. Harry Acker sat in a large, covered box that was tied to the roof of the house. A rope hung down the side and went into the kitchen window. As soon as Harry saw a rider approaching, he was to pull the rope. One of the Bar-X men in the hayloft of the barn was also on the lookout.

Father O'Brien was at the McTavish farm. He, too, had a couple of good riders with fast horses in the barn. Buckets of sand and water were positioned on the first floor of the house. His men stared out into the gently falling snow, looking for an approaching rider.

At the Dolinskis', Sheriff Tate had his team ready in case the arsonist targeted that house. Mrs. Dolinski heard the three rings of the church bell and informed Sheriff Tate.

"Three bells, men," called the sheriff. "One of the suspects has left Riverton and is heading east."

Back at the Donatellis' house, Harry Acker grasped the rope in anticipation of seeing a rider.

At the McTavish farm, one of the Bar-X men heard the bells and told Father O'Brien.

"How many rings?" asked the priest.

"Three," said the ranch hand. "I waited until they repeated the rings before I signaled you."

"Good," said Father O'Brien. "I'll alert the men."

"What do we do now?" asked Buck.

"We've done our part of the plan," Audrey replied. "Now we go home and wait."

Brad and Buck closed up the church while Audrey and Wilma Sue got the horses. They mounted, left the churchyard, and headed out of town.

"Since we're riding double, let's go slowly," said Brad.

"Brad Benton," said Wilma Sue, her nose raised and with a disdainful look, "are you implying our horse is so old that it can't go faster than a walk?" Brad looked at her with a bewildered furrowing of his eyebrows.

"What she means," explained Audrey, "is that we should let the horses trot. Isn't that right?"

"Yes," chuckled Wilma Sue.

"I'm missing something," said Buck.

"I'll tell you about it when we get home," Audrey promised. "Nana said she would have some oatmeal cookies ready for us."

"Well, in that case, let's trot," said Brad, gently pressing Ebony's flanks.

The horses trotted at a comfortable pace the rest of the way to the Benton house. When they reached the corral, Brad and Buck unsaddled and wiped down the horses while Wilma Sue and Audrey went into the house.

"Good timing. The cookies just came out of the oven." Mrs. Benton lifted the cookies off the pan and placed them on a wooden cooling rack.

"We popped them into the oven soon as we heard the church bell," said their grandmother. "Tea will be ready in a minute. Does anybody want hot chocolate instead?"

"I do," Buck responded as he came in the back door with Brad.

"Sit down and tell us all about it," insisted Mrs. Benton. "I know the reverend said you couldn't use names, so suspect is fine."

"Wilma Sue and I saw our suspect leave and head south," Buck began.

"Then he turned east," continued Wilma Sue. "That's when we signaled Brad."

"That was about ten o'clock," recalled Audrey. "The

Riverton Hotel was putting out the lamps in their dining room."

"So we all hurried over to the church and rang the bell," said Brad.

"I guess we'll have to wait until morning to find out what happened," sighed Mrs. Benton resignedly.

"I'll be happy if we don't have another fire," said their grandmother. "Any fire is bad, but it's worse when a fire is deliberate."

"Why would anyone want to hurt others like that?" wondered Wilma Sue.

"The man that set the fires is suffering also," remarked Mrs. Benton.

"What do you mean?" asked Buck.

"He's been hurt, and this is his twisted way of getting even."

"That's all fine and good," debated Brad, "but who hurt him? How was he hurt?"

"That's what the reverend needs to know," replied his grandmother. "When he finds out, he can help the arsonist."

"Then that's why he keeps asking the arsonist to come see him," said Audrey.

"If the arsonist will talk to the reverend or Father O'Brien, they may find a way to help relieve the pain," their grandmother explained. "When the pain is gone, his need to hurt others by setting fires will fade."

"A fire-crazy man would stay and watch the fires," said Mrs. Benton. "He doesn't; he just rides away. That's why we believe he starts the fires out of hatred."

"Did the reverend tell you this?" asked Wilma Sue.

"He and Father O'Brien stopped by last week, and we discussed the fires," said Nana.

Wilma Sue stifled a yarn. "I'm so exhausted, I'm going to fall asleep sitting in this chair."

"I see that everyone is doing the nod," commented Mrs. Benton. "So, it's time to go to bed. Audrey, you and Wilma Sue are sharing your bed. Is that right?"

"Yes, Ma."

"Buck, you take the guestroom," said Mrs. Benton. "You and Brad would never fit in the same bed."

"Thank you," Buck bowed deeply. "It is an honor to have use of the bed in which Running Bear has slept."

"Oh, Buck," giggled Audrey. "Now you're talking like him."

"It would be nice to follow in Running Bear's footsteps," said their grandmother. "He's a good man."

Wilma Sue and Audrey climbed the stairs to the bedroom.

"I am really tired," groaned Wilma Sue. "How about you?"

"I'll be asleep as soon as my head hits the pillow," said Audrey as she took off her boots and sweater.

"Will Brad want to sleep in tomorrow?" Wilma Sue inquired.

"I hope so," sighed Audrey as she pulled the covers up and dropped her head on her pillow. "I hope so."

Wilma Sue gazed out the window at the falling snow. "Morning will come soon enough. I'm going to sleep."

"Me, too, good night."

Brad and Buck stood in the doorway to the guestroom. Buck leaned against the doorframe.

"I never thought I'd be helping you and Audrey on one of your adventures."

"And I never imagined I'd be attempting to find someone who tried to kill me by burning my house. It's hard to believe that this man knows me."

"It's an unsettling predicament. I don't envy you," Buck admitted.

"I'm not happy about it, either," said Brad.

"Maybe one of the teams will capture the arsonist tonight," said Buck. "But for now, let's get some sleep. I'm bushed. Please remember to wake me when you get up."

"I'll probably be up at dawn," said Brad. "That's when Nana goes downstairs to start breakfast."

"Good. I need to get home first thing. I've got my chores to do." Buck entered the guest room and closed the door.

Brad withdrew to his room, sat on the edge of the bed, and took off his boots and crawled under the covers. As he drifted off to sleep, he thought to himself, *maybe one of the teams will capture the arsonist tonight. If they do, tomorrow we'll find out who he is.*

CHAPTER 11
CHRISTMAS

Saturday morning, 18 December: The sunlight streaming through her bedroom window roused Audrey as she turned over and bumped into someone. Startled, Audrey sat up in bed and was momentarily blinded by the brightness.

"Audrey," murmured Wilma Sue, squinting to see. "Is something wrong?"

"Uh, no," Audrey responded, rubbing her eyes. "I usually don't wake up this late, and the sun is so bright."

"We'd better get up," said Wilma Sue. "Brad and Buck have probably already gotten up, eaten breakfast, and saddled the horses."

Just then Brad tapped on Audrey's door. "Rise and shine! Buck and I have already eaten and saddled the horses. We're supposed to be at Reverend Wesley's house by nine o'clock."

"I was kidding about that," said Wilma Sue. "I really didn't think it would be true."

Audrey laughed. "As soon as I saw the sunlight, I knew Brad was already up and ready. And we do have a nine o'clock meeting."

Audrey and Wilma Sue quickly got dressed, splashed

126

water on their faces, brushed their hair, and went downstairs to the kitchen.

"Your breakfast will be ready in two shakes," said Nana. "I started the pancakes when Brad went up to knock on your door."

"Thanks," said Audrey.

"Does Brad always get up with the rooster?" asked Wilma Sue.

"Ever since he got Ebony," replied Nana. "He gets up and feeds the horses. If he's up before I am, he starts the fires too."

Audrey poured two large glasses of milk and set them on the table while her grandmother served the pancakes.

Audrey said grace and put a couple of pancakes on her plate as Wilma Sue took an egg and some bacon.

"When you and your brother return from meeting with the reverend, I want a detailed account of what happened last night," implored their grandmother. "None of that 'not much', you hear?"

"Yes, Nana," Audrey grinned.

"I have a shopping list for you while you're out."

"I'll pick up your things when we drop off Wilma Sue at the general store," replied Audrey.

After breakfast, they mounted the horses and headed to Reverend Wesley's.

"I hope nobody's house burned last night," said Wilma Sue.

"If the suspect tried, maybe one of the Bar-X men roped him before he could throw the bottle," Brad suggested.

"We'll know in a few minutes," said Buck. "There are already three horses at the reverend's house."

Brad knocked on the door. Mrs. Wesley opened and led them into the kitchen. Reverend Wesley, Father O'Brien, and Sheriff Tate were already there.

"No one came to any of the three houses last night," the reverend informed them.

"But we saw the suspect leave and ride south, then turn east," disputed Buck.

"It was about ten o'clock," added Audrey.

"I'm not sure what happened, but I'll go ask some questions," said Sheriff Tate. "Everyone else can go home. Remember, we can't talk to anyone about last night. Don't mention any names; don't even hint at what we did."

"If the arsonist tries again, we want to be able to surprise him," explained Father O'Brien. "And hopefully, we'll capture him."

"All right, everyone," said the sheriff, "let's meet here at two o'clock. I'll be able to tell you what I find out, and then we can plan what our next step will be."

"Wilma Sue, I'll drop you at your father's store," offered Buck.

"Nana gave us a shopping list," said Audrey, "so we'll ride with you to the store."

"I'll see everyone at two o'clock," the reverend reminded them.

"Buck, Wilma Sue, thanks for helping," said Father O'Brien.

"Pa is expecting me to help him this morning," Wilma Sue stood up. "I've got to get going."

"My Pa is expecting me, too," said Buck. "I've still got my chores."

"We'll see you at two, Reverend," said Brad as Mrs. Wesley opened the front door for them.

The four of them mounted the horses and headed for the general store.

"Brad, Audrey, thanks for the warm bed and the food," said Buck as they turned onto Main Street.

"Thanks for helping us watch the suspects," replied Audrey.

Buck stopped in front of the general store and helped Wilma Sue down from his horse. "Thanks for the ride, Buck. I'll see you tomorrow."

"Let's fill our shopping list and get home," said Audrey as they entered the store. "Nana will be looking out the front window for us in a little bit."

"You're lucky to have her living with you," said Wilma Sue, gathering the items on the list.

Brad looked at her a moment. "I never thought of it that way. I'm happy she lives with us, but I've never realized how fortunate we are to have her here."

A few minutes later, Wilma Sue had filled their order and totalled the bill. Audrey paid, and Brad scooped up the bag.

"We'll see you tomorrow," said Audrey.

The ride home was pleasantly uneventful. Brad turned the horses into the corral but left their saddles on.

"We'll be leaving again in a few hours," said Brad as they walked toward the back door.

"There won't be much to tell Nana," said Audrey, opening the door.

As they had promised, Brad and Audrey recounted the meeting at the reverend's house that morning.

"I'm pleased to hear that there wasn't another fire," declared their grandmother. "Thank you for picking up the items on my list. You'd best do your homework while I fix lunch. Your father will be home shortly, and the next thing you know, it will be time to meet with the reverend again."

"Thanks, Nana. Good idea," said Audrey.

It was a few minutes before two when Brad and Audrey arrived at the reverend's house. Mrs. Wesley let them in and told them to go into the kitchen.

"Good afternoon, Brad, Audrey," Reverend Wesley patted them.

"Bob was just starting to tell me a story," said Father O'Brien.

"I'll start over. The evangelist, Dwight Moody, was visiting the last town on his evangelical tour in Illinois. Moody sat down on a bench in the town square to catch up on his correspondence. A young boy came through the park, and Moody asked him how to get to the post office. Moody introduced himself as an evangelist. He said he could show the boy and his family how to get into Heaven and offered the lad four front row seats to that evening's revival meeting. The boy thanked him, but refused the reserved seats. Moody, rather perplexed, asked him why. The boy hung his head and replied that Moody really didn't want to know. Moody persisted, and finally the lad said that if you don't even know the way to the post office, how can you possibly tell people how to get to Heaven?"

When the laughter subsided, Father O'Brien said, "I'll have to tell you some that I heard at the seminary."

Mrs. Wesley heard a knock at the front door. "They'll have to wait; that must be the sheriff."

Sheriff Tate joined them in the kitchen to relate his news. "I talked to Alex at the stable this morning. He said the suspect rented a horse for the weekend. Told him he was going to visit a friend. Alex asked him about the friend, but the suspect changed the subject. Alex knows better than to pry, so he thanked him for his business and said he'd see him Monday."

"I spoke with Mr. Bevins," said the reverend. "He hasn't heard anything about a fire last night."

"I had lunch with David Acker," said Father O'Brien. "He and his staff haven't heard anything about a fire either."

"For some reason, the arsonist didn't strike last night," remarked the reverend. "He may have known that we were watching him."

"It's also possible he may be losing his hatred," suggested Father O'Brien.

"We all want that to happen," affirmed Audrey.

"We'll just have to wait for the next snow and then implement the plan again," Sheriff Tate concluded.

"I agree," said the reverend.

"We'll tell Buck and Wilma Sue," offered Brad.

"Let us close with a prayer, and then we can enjoy a slice of my wife's applesauce cake," said the reverend.

Reverend Wesley said a short prayer, and his wife

passed out the cake while Father O'Brien and Audrey poured tea and coffee.

Friday, 24 December: Reverend Wesley, his wife, and Father O'Brien were in the Wesley kitchen eating lunch.

"Another piece of corn bread, Father?" asked Mrs. Wesley.

"Thank you, but no," replied Father O'Brien. "You can't bribe a Roman Catholic priest into agreeing with a Protestant minister, even if he is your husband."

"I hadn't thought of that," chuckled Reverend Wesley. "Offer him two pieces. I need to win this debate."

"I know you want to help this man," said Father O'Brien, "but I don't think you should invite him to stay in your home overnight."

"I understand," the reverend assured him, "but I've already discussed it with Martha, and she's agreed to have him spend the night with us."

"I'll do my part. I want you to succeed, but, I think it's very risky, especially since your wife is with child," Father O'Brien added.

"I appreciate your concern," said Reverend Wesley, "but I think we're getting through to him. This act of kindness and trust may be what it takes to save him."

At two o'clock, Jake Jackson lit the fires in the church stoves. They were heating up nicely when the Riverton families started to arrive for the Christmas pageant. They came by wagon, buggy, foot, and horseback. Sunday school teachers reminded the children what they were supposed to do in their roles. Reverend Wesley was running around like a horse with a burr under his saddle trying to make sure that things would go smoothly. Father O'Brien served as his assistant, using small pieces of colored paper to mark the appropriate pages of the Bible. When everything was finally ready, Reverend Wesley asked Abby Benton to play the prelude.

The joyous Christmas music quickly quieted the congregation.

"The reverend's ready, Abby," whispered Jake from his deacon's chair. "Start the opening hymn."

Mrs. Benton began the opening hymn, and Reverend Wesley's voice boomed from the back of the church. As was his custom, he strode down the aisle on the second verse, turned, and faced the congregation.

He read a passage from the Bible and said, "The Christmas Pageant is today's sermon. It tells the story of the birth of Christ far better than I can." He nodded toward the piano and the Sunday school classes began to sing "O Little Town of Bethlehem." Angus McTavish played the part of Joseph, Gina Donatelli the part of Mary. Brad, Audrey, Buck, and Wilma Sue stood at the side ready to prompt the children, but prompting wasn't necessary. The pageant was a success, despite the tummy pillow falling out of Mary's dress as she entered the stable. Gina simply stopped, picked up the pillow, and stuffed it back up under the front of her oversized dress.

After the performance, Reverend Wesley made his announcements. "Father O'Brien will offer Christmas

Mass at nine o'clock tomorrow morning. I'll have our Christmas service at half past ten."

He said the closing prayer and added, "Lord, we thank you for helping the arsonist stop setting fires. Please have him seek understanding and guidance from Father O'Brien or myself. Please let us get through this winter without another fire. Amen."

Mrs. Benton played the closing hymn, and folks congratulated the children on their splendid performance of the Christmas story.

Brad put his hand on Arturo Donatelli's shoulder and said, "Very good performance, Arturo."

"Thanks, Brad. We did what you told us to do."

"Wilma Sue," declared Mr. Benton. "You did an excellent job coaching the mother of Jesus."

"Thank you," replied Wilma Sue, blushing slightly. "I'm sorry her pillow fell out."

"That just made the pageant more memorable," Mr. Benton assured her. "Don't worry about it."

"Ah, there are my three wise men." Father O'Brien clapped his hands together. "Excellent job, Brad, Buck, and Harry. And Harry, extend my thanks to your father for letting you help us out with the pageant."

"I will, Father," replied Harry.

"Happy Hanukkah, too," winked Father O'Brien.

A broad smile spread across Harry's face, and he responded, "Merry Christmas to you, Father."

Thirty minutes later, Reverend Wesley, Father O'Brien, and William Brock were the only ones remaining in the church. Father O'Brien checked the stove and joined the other two at the front.

"William," said Reverend Wesley. "Thanks for helping with the scenery."

"Uh, you're welcome, Reverend," stammered William. "I'm glad I could help."

"And, William," continued the reverend, "Martha and I would like you and Father O'Brien to stay with us tonight, on Christmas Eve, and share Christmas dinner with us tomorrow. May I tell her that you accept the invitation?"

William's jaw dropped open in disbelief. His eyes widened as he raised his head. "Well, yes, Reverend, I'd like that. Thank you for inviting me."

"Good," said the reverend. "Then it's settled. Help us close up the church, and we'll go home. Martha always makes something nice for supper on Christmas Eve. You do have an appetite, don't you?"

"I certainly do," William assured him.

"Good. I wouldn't want you to hurt her feelings by not eating."

The three men departed, walking through the gently falling snow toward the reverend's home. Stores were closed, the streets vacant. The soft crunching of the snow under their boots and the muted haze of the setting sun softly shining through the veil of snow surrounded them with an aura of Christmas Eve tranquility.

"Father O'Brien, what did you mean when you said 'Happy Hanukkah' to Harry Acker?" asked William.

"The Ackers are Jewish," explained Father O'Brien. "They don't celebrate Christmas. Hanukkah has no relation to Christmas, but it does occur right about the same time."

"Hanukkah celebrates freedom and the Maccabee

tribe's victory over their oppressors in the 2nd century A.D. The Greeks and Assyrians had prohibited them from worshipping God in the Hebrew tradition."

"Centuries later, in order to study the Torah, their Bible, Jewish men would gather in the woods. If soldiers approached them, the men would start playing with a top, called a dreidel," added Reverend Wesley.

"The word Hanukkah means dedication. Jews celebrate the reclaiming of the Hebrew temple in Jerusalem from the Assyrians," continued Father O'Brien. "They had cleaned the temple and went to light the temple lamps, but they could only find enough sanctified oil to burn for one day."

"That one-day supply of oil lasted eight days, long enough for them to find more oil," added Reverend Wesley. "I call that divine intervention. Here's my home," as he gestured to the house on their right.

"You have a marvelous wife, Bob," said Father O'Brien. "What did you do to deserve her?"

"Really, it was quite simple," replied the reverend. "I asked the Lord for a wife who would help me do His work."

Reverend Wesley opened the front door and motioned Father O'Brien and John to enter. The mouthwatering aroma of fresh bread and beef stew spurred their appetites, while Mrs. Wesley's voice, caroling in the kitchen, reminded the men of angels heralding the birth of the Christ child.

"We're home," the reverend called to his wife. "William accepted our invitation and is with us."

"I'll take the coats," offered Father O'Brien, hanging

the reverend's on one of the wall pegs. "Yours too, William."

William removed his coat, hesitantly handed it to Father O'Brien, and then followed the reverend into the kitchen. His eyes peered around the room. In the center was a large round table with six chairs. Gingham curtains covered the window. On the kitchen range were a kettle and a large pot of stew. Three golden loaves of bread were cooling on the wooden counter.

"Have a seat, gentlemen," said Mrs. Wesley. "Bob, would you please fill the soup bowls while I take care of the bread?"

"Of course," he responded and ladled stew into the first bowl.

"Nothing fancy," declared Mrs. Wesley, "just good, simple food." She cut a loaf of bread into large slices and set it on the table. As the reverend was filling the last bowl with steaming stew, she went out the back door, opened a box, and returned with a large brick of sour cream butter.

As soon as everyone was seated, Mrs. Wesley said, "Bob."

They bowed their heads as the reverend said grace. William lowered his head also, but raised it just enough to peer at the others. He studied Mrs. Wesley's peaceful face during the prayer. When the reverend said 'Amen,' William looked over and saw Father O'Brien smiling.

"Dig in," urged Reverend Wesley, picking up his spoon.

Father O'Brien took a bite, opened his eyes wide, and exclaimed, "This stew is delicious!"

"There's more in the pot," said the reverend. "There is plenty for seconds."

"It tastes just like the stew they served when I was in seminary," recalled the priest, "only better."

"It should," chuckled Mrs. Wesley. "It's their recipe, and how I got it is a secret!"

"This is much better than any soup I've ever tasted," said William, adding to the compliments.

"Wait until you taste the bread," advised Father O'Brien.

After supper, Father O'Brien washed the dishes, the reverend dried, and Mrs. Wesley put them away in the cabinet. William went out to the back porch and refilled the woodbox and the kindling bucket. When the kitchen chores were done, they retired to the small parlor and sat in front of the fireplace.

"So, William, do you have any questions about the Christmas pageant?" asked Reverend Wesley.

"I know it's about the birth of Jesus," replied William, "but not much else."

"Aren't you the lucky one," Father O'Brien grinned. "Bob tells the story better than anyone I've ever heard, but don't let my bishop know that."

Reverend Wesley proceeded to share the story of Jesus. William perched forward in his chair, his eyes riveted on the reverend. Father O'Brien sat back and viewed the two of them. Mrs. Wesley came in, settled down in her chair, and placed her hands on her swelling abdomen. She smiled as the baby in her womb kicked and punched at his small enclosure.

At the Benton house, Christmas Eve supper consisted of venison sandwiches, canned peaches, coffee, and tea. After the meal, Brad filled the woodboxes and checked the fire buckets.

"Brad," said Audrey, "I'm worried about Reverend Wesley."

"Why?"

"One of the suspects is spending the night with him," replied Audrey. "He's the one that rode out of town during the snow last Friday night."

"I understand why you're concerned, but I'm sure Reverend Wesley knows what he is doing. Plus, Father O'Brien will be with them. The arsonist set the fires anonymously. If he had wanted to kill his victims, he could have shot them right away, or he could have shot them while they fought the flames. I don't think the arsonist is a killer. He is very angry about something and wants to get even. He wants to hurt people. If we knew why, we might be able to convince him to stop setting the fires."

"You may be right," said Audrey. "If he is the arsonist, Reverend Wesley is the one to help him see that setting fires will not help him get even; it will only fuel his hate."

Brad looked around and then whispered to his sister, "Come up to my room. Help me wrap Pa's Christmas present."   Brad went to his room, and a few minutes later Audrey followed. She quietly opened Brad's door, slipped inside, and eased the door shut. Her brother was pulling a box out from under his bed.

"When did the hat come in?"

"Earlier this week," answered Brad. "I picked it up

when I took Nana to the general store on Wednesday. Did you get Ma's present?"

"Yes, I've already wrapped it."

From behind Brad's chest of drawers, he pulled out a giant sheet of white paper that Wilma Sue had gotten for them. Audrey took a regular pencil and a red pencil and started drawing on the wrapping paper. Brad watched in amazement as his sister sketched some holly leaves and then added some red berries.

"You're so artistic," he said, watching his sister with admiration.

"Thank you," Audrey responded. "I may have artistic ability, but you sure have a way with horses."

When she finished decorating the paper, they wrapped the hat for their father.

"The hat he's got now had some holes in it even before Duke Badger took his good one along with his coat and boots," observed Brad. "He really needs a new hat."

"I can't wait to see Ma's face when she opens her present. I wrote a letter to the organist at the Denver Community Church about some prelude music," said Audrey. "He sent me the names and prices of two prelude collections for piano. Jim Bates bought the music for me when he went to Denver just after Thanksgiving."

"He picked up Nana's present, too," said Brad. "I got her that new cookbook she read about in *Harper's*. We'd better get back downstairs. Ma will want us to sing Christmas carols, and Pa said he's going to read Charles Dickens's book, *A Christmas Carol*."

"Pa has read us that story every Christmas for years," remembered Audrey. "It's good; Pa says it's a classic."

140

They went downstairs and placed the gifts under the tree.

Their mother came out of the kitchen a few minutes later and went to the piano. She started playing "I Heard the Bells on Christmas Day."

"That's one of the new carols," remarked their grandmother. "It was written before the Civil War ended."

"1864 is the date on the music; that's one year before the Civil War ended" said their mother. "Now let's sing."

They sang several carols, concluding with *What Child is This?* They looked expectantly at Harold Benton after they finished.

"I guess that means it's time," he said as he lit the lantern hanging over his chair.

The women snuggled up in their chairs with quilts wrapped around their legs. Brad and Audrey brought down their pillows and blankets. Brad lit a second lantern and curled up in front of the stove beside his sister. Their father sat down in his chair, opened the book, and began to read.

"Dickens calls each section of his book a stave, rather than a chapter," said their father. "Stave One, Marley's Ghost. Marley was dead, to begin with. There is no doubt whatever about that..."

After the first stave, Brad got up and said, "Let me add some wood to the fire. I get cold just listening to Scrooge's stinginess."

Brad added a large piece of wood to the fire and then settled down as his father began reading stave two.

Sometime later, when he had finished stave five, their mother called for a break. "Don't start the last stave until I serve the cookies and cider."

"Hot apple cider?" Mr. Benton's eyes lit up.

"Yes," said Nana. "Hot apple cider. We haven't had any for a long time. I even added some cinnamon sticks."

"That explains the wonderful smell," noted Brad.

"Everyone remain right where you are," ordered their grandmother. "We'll bring the cookies and cider in here."

They returned in a few minutes with five large mugs of piping hot cider and a plate piled with cookies. Mr. Benton, the first to be served, quickly devoured a couple of cookies before resuming the story.

"We're ready," said Audrey.

"Stave five," he began. "The End of It. Yes! And the bedpost was his own..."

He paused several times during the last stave to sip his cider and nibble a cookie. Brad and Audrey were on their backs, their hands behind their heads, resting on their pillows and blankets.

"And so, as Tiny Tim observed, God bless Us, Every One!" concluded Mr. Benton, closing the book and draining his mug of cider.

"I've heard you read that every Christmas, Pa, but it's still a great story," professed Audrey.

"I'm glad you like it," replied her father.

"What about Charles Dickens?" asked Brad. "What do you know about him?"

"I've followed newspaper and magazine articles about him," he said. "Dickens wrote *A Christmas Carol* in December of 1843. My father bought the book and read it to my brother and me every Christmas from the time I was eight. That would have been 1848. Dickens was a Christian, and his books reflected his concerns about the cruelty of some of society's actions. Debtor's prison is a good example. Charles's father spent about four months in prison because he owed money."

"The Marxists thought he shared their goals. They tried to get him to be their spokesman because he worked with others to eliminate the inhumane treatment and cruel actions of his government," added their mother.

"The ideals of Marxism are peaceful, but unfortunately, the greed of many of its leaders profaned the original goals," explained their father. "Everyone is supposedly equal, except the leaders who, of course, are more equal."

"More equal means they take what they want," said their grandmother. "Corrupt Marxists are like the Anarchists. They want to destroy the government so they can control the country. Once in control, they can take what they want and do anything they wish."

"But if the Anarchists oppose authority, why would they want the authority of control?" asked Brad.

"So they can do what they want," explained their mother. "So they can enslave you and take what is yours with no fear of reprisal. They're like Duke Badger."

"So the Marxists wanted Dickens to be their spokesman," said Brad. "I suppose Dickens said no."

"That he did," their father confirmed, "but he also worked to eliminate the cruel laws of the government and brought about some reforms. He died ten years ago, in 1870."

"This is another simple question that became a whole history lesson," Audrey grinned.

"Just like that question we asked last summer about the Civil War," remembered Brad.

"Your answers may be long, Pa," said Audrey, "but we learn so much from them."

"Yes," agreed Brad.

"My, it's late," said their father as he looked at his pocket watch. "Time to hit the hay."

Audrey followed Brad up the stairs to their bedrooms. The adults lingered in the kitchen finishing the last of the cider.

Audrey leaned against the door frame to her brother's room. "Brad," I can't help worrying about the reverend."

"You're concerned because a suspect is staying with them tonight?"

"Yes."

"I'm worried too," said Brad. "Tomorrow, we can ask Reverend Wesley how the evening went."

"You're right; let's get some sleep."

CHAPTER 12
CHRISTMAS DAY

Saturday, 25 December: Brad heard his grandmother go down the stairs to the kitchen. He quietly got up, dressed, rinsed his face, and then combed his hair before joining her.

"Morning, Nana," greeted Brad in a soft voice. "Merry Christmas!"

"Merry Christmas to you, too," she said, kissing her grandson on the cheek.

"I'll start the fire in the parlor stove," he said.

Brad entered the other room and looked around. He thought of the fire that had caused so much damage weeks earlier. Fortunately, the piano had escaped the flames. So had his father's favorite chair and the oak table that Harold had made for Abby. The ceiling still bore black smoke smudges despite Nana's scrubbing. She had to get rid of the rug that had been in the center of the floor; the blaze had burned a large hole as well as many smaller holes. Broken glass, sand, and water ruined what the fire hadn't.

Brad put some newspaper, kindling, and small sticks of wood in the stove and struck a match. As soon as the fire was going strong, he opened the stove and added several medium-sized pieces of wood and one large piece.

Audrey watched him close the stove door and then said, "Merry Christmas, Brad. I heard Ma and Pa stirring when I came downstairs."

Brad turned to look at his sister and the presents under the tree. "Merry Christmas, Audrey."

"You're very quiet, Brad. Is something wrong?"

"I was thinking about our search for Pa. I thought that was the most dangerous thing we'd ever faced. Now, it's the arsonist. We've put out two fires, flames that could have killed us if we had started fighting them even half a minute later. Looking back on it, those fires were a lot more dangerous than capturing the Big Foot Gang, searching for Pa, hiding from Duke Badger, and surviving that blizzard. This is even scarier than capturing Garth Pugh."

"You're a little young to be so nostalgic. Besides, I'm the one that broke Garth Pugh's jaw," she said, suppressing a laugh.

Brad grinned and said, "It sure was hard on him when the other prisoners found out his jaw had been broken by a girl. Sheriff Tate said they teased him about it incessantly until Running Bear explained to all of them how fortunate Garth was that you only broke his jaw."

Audrey thought about saving their lives by breaking Garth's jaw with her rifle barrel. Garth had freed his hands, taken their father's pistol, and knocked her father off his horse. vividly recalled Garth swinging his pistol towards her as she stood in the stirrups of her horse to smash the barrel of her rifle barrel into his jaw.

"Audrey," said Brad as he gently poked his sister, "what are you thinking?"

"Now you're acting like the Brad Benton I've always known," she said, grabbing her brother's hand. "Come into the kitchen. Let's help Nana start Christmas dinner before we go to the Christmas service."

Brad went to the wood shed to retrieve the roast Len Reno had brought the previous day. Audrey brought up some carrots, potatoes, and apples from the root cellar.

"I've made some tea to go with the jam and bread," offered their grandmother. "That should hold you until Christmas dinner, which should be around noon."

"Thanks, Nana," said Audrey as she took a seat at the table.

"We'll say hello to the reverend for you," said Brad reaching for another slice of bread.

"It was very kind for the two of you to offer your help with his Christmas morning service," remarked their father, entering the kitchen.

"We're concerned about him," Audrey confessed. "He asked one of the suspects to spend the night at his home and share Christmas dinner with him."

He nodded. "Sometimes showing trust, sharing, or just being kind erases hate. Reverend Wesley is a very good judge of people. He wouldn't have taken the risk if he didn't believe he could succeed."

"We know, Pa," said Audrey. "But we're still worried about it."

"It's good to be concerned, but you must also have faith in what the reverend's trying to accomplish. And be sure and say hello to William Brock; he may not be the arsonist. There was no fire the night that he left in the snow storm.

"The more I think about it, I don't think he is the arsonist," revealed Audrey. "He's polite, well-mannered, and," she paused, "well, I like him. How do you feel about him, Brad?"

"I'm not sure he's the arsonist either. I suspect the other man; he doesn't talk much, and he's afraid of Sheriff Tate."

"Goodness, you're going to be late if you don't get going," admonished their father. "Reverend Wesley is counting on you."

The Wesleys and their guests sat around the kitchen table. Father O'Brien finished his cup of coffee, looked across the table, and said, "William, would you please assist me with my service?"

"Why, uh, sure," he replied. "I don't understand very much of this church stuff, but I'll help however I can."

"I'll explain what we're doing," assured the priest. "Mostly, I just need an extra set of hands."

William Brock watched Father O'Brien don his black clerical coat, followed by a long wool overcoat and hat. Once outside, he asked, "Why the black shirt, white collar, and black coat?"

"A soldier wears a uniform as a symbol of his devotion to the service of his country. A Catholic Priest wears his uniform--the black shirt, white collar, and black coat as a symbol of his devotion to the service of the Lord."

"And the cross?"

"That symbolizes the crucifixion of Jesus for our sins,"

explained Father O'Brien as he opened the front door of the church. "Jesus was sentenced to death by a small group of Jewish rabbis in Jerusalem that were members of what was called the Great Sanhedrin. Pontius Pilate, a Roman official, claimed there was no evidence to justify the death penalty. After repeated demands by the corrupt members of the Great Sanhedrin and the increasingly strident demands of their mob, however, Pontius Pilate was faced with the possibility of a riot if he did not approve the death penalty. He finally gave permission for the execution of Jesus, but he told the rabbis, and their mob, that he washed his hands of the whole affair. He even physically washed his hands in front of the people to symbolize his disapproval of their demands. Jesus was nailed to a large cross. Scholars believe it took many hours for him to die."

"What did he do to be executed?" William inquired as he built a fire in the stove.

"He displeased some of the religious leaders," replied Father O'Brien. "Some members of the Great Sanhedrin were making money by using the temple as a marketplace. Jesus ran those merchants out of the temple. He exposed their dishonesty and he reduced their illegal income. Some Jews said that Jesus was innocent, but they were silenced. Other members of the Great Sanhedrin were not even informed of the trial. It was an illegal trial in that all the members of the Great Sanhedrin were not present, but Pontius Pilate did not know that. Many people liked Jesus, and he did great things for the common man. They went to Jesus for help rather than to those religious leaders who lost their illegal income. That's why some of the leaders felt threatened by Jesus. He threatened their power. Power and greed have been the seeds of man's destruction since the beginning of time."

"Then he didn't deserve to be executed?"

"No, he didn't. Pontius Pilate, the Roman governor in Jerusalem, told the religious leaders that Jesus had done nothing wrong."

"But they killed him anyway?"

"Yes. He was a threat to those few dishonest religious leaders in Jerusalem. His death, however, forged the creation of Christianity, changing the world in ways no one could have believed possible."

"How did you learn all this?"

"By reading the Bible and going to Seminary," said Father O'Brien. "It's all in the Bible. Do you have a Bible?"

"No, my Pa told me it was a waste of time."

"Well, he has a right to his opinion, but I don't believe it is a waste of time," insisted Father O'Brien, laying out his vestments. "My parishioners will begin arriving in a few minutes. Why don't you sit in the chair by the piano and watch what I do? I'll explain it to you after the service."

"Uh, I'd like that, uh, Father. Yes, I'd like that. Let me add some wood to the fires before the people come."

Brad and Audrey finished their bread and jam, chatted with their parents, and put on their coats and headed for the barn. Blaze and Ebony came to Brad for their apples and were saddled.

150

"You trained them well with the apples," Audrey commented, putting on the bridles.

"It's a lot easier than chasing them," Brad grinned. "I'll race you to the road."

"Of course, Blaze should win this time. I only had one slice of bread as opposed to your two, so I'll weigh less," she teased.

Brad closed the gate and mounted Ebony. Audrey was ready and said, "On the count of three. One, two, three!"

The horses immediately broke into a gallop. Audrey started in the lead with Brad slowly gaining. By the time they reached the road, Blaze was ahead only by a neck.

They slowed to a trot for the rest of the ride. There had been a dusting of snow that night, and everything looked white and clean.

"Ebony must not be feeling well," Brad rationalized, "she was slower than usual."

"It could be that you're getting heavier," Audrey said, jabbing her brother. "I didn't say you're fat, I just said heavier."

Father O'Brien stood at the church door as his parishioners departed. The Donatellis were the last to leave, and he wished them a Merry Christmas. He closed the door and went to warm his hands by the stove as William added another piece of wood.

"I couldn't understand anything you said," he said. "What language was that?"

"It was Latin," replied the priest. "It's the universal

language of the Roman Catholic Church. All Catholic priests throughout the world conduct the mass, or service, in Latin."

"Reverend Wesley does his service in English," noted William.

"The protestant churches elected to conduct the service in the language of the people. Roman Catholics follow the guidance of Pope Leo XIII, who is the head of the Roman Catholic Church. The requirement for Latin may change in the future, but for now, the mass must be conducted in Latin."

"Good morning," said Reverend Wesley, entering through the side door. "William, thank you for helping Trevor this morning, it gave me some time with Martha. She doesn't feel well in the mornings, being with child and all."

"Morning, Bob," said Father O'Brien. "I hear some horses outside. Folks must be starting to arrive for your service."

"Trevor," suggested the reverend, "maybe you could take William into the alcove and explain the service to him; what you might call an instructional Mass."

William and Father O'Brien stood in a corner of the church as people entered. Outside, Brad and Audrey looped their reins over the hitching rail and climbed the front steps.

Brad opened the door saying, "After you, Audrey."

She entered, heard voices on her left and turned to see William and Father O'Brien.

"Good morning, William, Father," said Audrey, "Merry Christmas."

"Same to you, Audrey, Brad," Father O'Brien responded. William nodded his head in agreement.

Brad and Audrey went to the front of the church and sat in a pew next to Wilma Sue and her family. "Merry Christmas," said Brad softly.

"Merry Christmas," whispered Wilma Sue. "It snowed last night, but I don't think there was a fire."

Reverend Wesley walked to the front and opened with a brief prayer. He read some passages from the Bible and began his sermon. In the back of the church, Father O'Brien explained the service as it progressed.

"And now, our closing prayer," began Reverend Wesley.

The congregation was small but appreciative. The reverend stood in the back of the church after the service and thanked them for coming.

"Glad you could make it," Reverend Wesley said to Brad and Audrey. "I didn't expect you since you were here for the Christmas Eve service."

"We wanted to come. We've never been to a Christmas Day service, just the Christmas Eve service," divulged Audrey.

"And you had an opportunity to see if the church was still here?" replied the reverend, a twinkle in his eye.

Audrey blushed and said, "Well, that too."

"You're smothering our possible enemy with love," Brad commented as he grasped the reverend's hand.

"I'm glad you said possible enemy," said Reverend Wesley. "We don't know; we may never know who the real arsonist is."

"Well, we'll be back at three o'clock to begin the visitations," said Audrey.

"Good," nodded the reverend. "I'll see you then."

They mounted their horses and headed home. The horses pranced through the snow, enjoying the sun and the ride.

"Hungry?" asked Audrey.

"Of course; I didn't have much for breakfast. I'll survive, though. Christmas dinner is less than an hour from now."

Brad opened the corral gate, and they led the horses into the barn. After removing the saddles, they went into the house.

"Audrey," said Brad. "I don't know if you agree with me, but really I don't think William is the arsonist."

"I doubt he is, either."

They walked into the kitchen and were immediately struck with the aroma of roast and pumpkin pie.

"Welcome back," said their mother. "We're ready to open the presents; then we'll have dinner."

The Bentons gathered in the parlor, gathered around the Christmas tree and opened their gifts. Brad got a hunting knife and whetstone; Audrey received a new dress and a diary. Their grandmother was overjoyed with her cookbook, as was their mother with the two music books. Their father looked at his new hat and said he wasn't sure he wanted to wear it—-the old one brought back some marvelous memories.

"Oh, I have a lovely new tablecloth," exclaimed their mother opening another package.

Brad and Audrey spread the new cloth on the dining room table.

"It looks very nice," said Audrey. "Shall we set out the dishes?"

154

In a few minutes, the table was set, laden with food, and everyone was seated.

"Harold," said his wife.

He said grace, and the Bentons passed their plates. When everyone had been served, they began eating. Brad quickly finished his plate.

"It's good that the horses can relax until tomorrow," observed Mrs. Benton as her son took a second slice of roast.

"Not exactly," said Audrey with a sigh. "We need them to get to Reverend Wesley's visitations this afternoon."

The Wesleys, Father O'Brien, and William Brock all enjoyed Martha Wesley's Christmas dinner. Afterwards, there was an exchange of gifts.

"William, we have a present for you," said Reverend Wesley, handing a small package to him.

"I think it's something you want," added Father O'Brien. "We know it's something you need."

William opened the box and saw that it was a Bible. He looked at the gift, and then at Reverend Wesley, whose eyes were looking deeply into him. Father O'Brien smiled when William looked at him, as did Mrs. Wesley.

"No one has ever given me a Christmas present before," William admitted, a tear streaming down the side of his face. "I haven't given you anything."

"If you become a Christian, you will have given us a marvelous gift," replied Mrs. Wesley. "Besides, this is Christmas. This is a day to be thankful for; it's the day our Lord, Jesus Christ was born. It is a day to be happy, a day to enjoy."

"Thanks for sharing this day with us," said the reverend.

Brad and Audrey saddled their horses for the second time that day and headed to Riverton. When they reached the church, they saw Buck Hodges's horse and a long hay wagon with benches. Sarah Davis and her son were on the front steps of the church talking with Reverend Wesley.

Brad and Audrey dismounted and went to join them. Sarah saw them coming and waved.

"Merry Christmas, Mrs. Davis," called Brad. "We'll see you later this afternoon."

"Are we all here?" inquired the reverend. "Let's hop on the wagon and get started."

Brad and William helped the women climb onto the wagon. When everyone was seated, Jake Jackson gently slapped the reins. The two horses eased into their harnesses and started out of the churchyard.

In a few minutes they reached the first house, and Reverend Wesley announced, *"Hark! The Herald Angels Sing,* first verse only."

The group climbed off the wagon and started singing. Just before they finished, the front door opened and an elderly, frail lady peered out.

"Come in, come in," she insisted. The reverend led the group into her small house. "Please have some cookies." She studied Brad's face carefully and continued, "You're the young man that drove the stage I was on back to Riverton after Duke Badger shot the driver."

"Yes, ma'am," said Brad.

"And you're his sister," she continued, smiling at Audrey. "You two saved the driver's life after that terrible man shot him. He would have bled to death without your bandaging."

Before Audrey could respond, Reverend Wesley said, "Kathleen, we brought you a Christmas present."

"Why, thank you," she said, taking the package.

"Go ahead," he prodded, "open it."

Her gnarled fingers unwrapped the package and pulled out some needles, thread, a pair of scissors, several parcels of brightly colored cloth, and a pair of spectacles. Her eyes opened wide in delight.

"Oh, thank you!" she cried, embracing the reverend. "Now I can make some dresses for my granddaughters."

"Thank you for the cookies," the reverend responded. "We've got to leave now; we have quite a few more stops to make. Merry Christmas."

The group got back in the wagon, and Jake drove them to the next person on the visitation list. After about an hour, they only had one more stop to make. Jake halted the wagon in front of the boarding house, the group went up the steps, and Sarah Davis greeted them on the porch.

"There's an old man in the parlor. His name is Samuel," Sarah informed them. "He's a Civil War veteran who served with General Garfield. He doesn't have long to live; Doc Adams said he only had a few months left. He's losing weight rapidly, no matter how much he eats. Samuel has no relatives. Riverton and the church are his family."

The group entered the living room. Samuel was seated in a rocking chair, slowly rocking, his eyes closed.

"*The Holly and the Ivy,*" said Father O'Brien in a soft voice as he hummed the starting pitch.

When they finished the carol, Samuel's face broke into a big smile. Sarah introduced him, and Reverend Wesley patted him on the back.

"I always loved that carol," remarked Samuel. "It's one of my favorites. My ma sang it every Christmas when I was a child, but she died of consumption when I was about twelve. I worked on a neighbor's farm for a few years, then headed out west. I owned a freight business for a while and sold that when I got too old to run the business; been living off the proceeds ever since."

"Here's some coffee, Samuel," offered Sarah. "Would you like a slice of the pie Maggie made today?"

"Sure would," replied Samuel. "You know how much I like her pies."

Sarah handed him a cup of coffee and slice of pie. He took a couple of bites, and then looked at Brad.

"You're Brad Benton, aren't you?" he asked.

"Yes, sir," said Brad. "And this is my sister, Audrey."

"I know most of the folks, but I've never seen you up close, just from the porch or through the window. You're the type of young man this country needs."

"Thank you," said Brad, shuffling his feet nervously.

"You and your sister found your father and rescued him from certain death after that terrible outlaw, Duke Badger, kidnapped him and then shot him. I'm glad Marshal Benton put an end to that man. Was that marshal any relation to you?"

"Yes, sir, our uncle."

"Well, when you see him, give him my thanks," said Samuel. "Years ago, that Duke Badger held me up, took my money and my horse. Then he shot me in the leg and laughed as he rode away. He left me to die in the mountains. I would have died too, if an Indian hadn't found me. He put me on the back of his horse and took me to his village. They nursed me back to health, and when I was well enough to travel, the Indians took me to an Army fort."

"Eat your pie, Samuel," reminded Sarah.

"Pie? Yes, my pie," recalled Samuel, taking another bite. "Thanks for singing that carol, it meant a lot to me. Of course, I'll be with the Lord shortly; then I'll hear real nice music - the music of the angels."

"We've got to go now, Samuel," said Reverend Wesley. "I'll stop by tomorrow."

Joined by Mrs. Davis, the group buttoned up their coats and left the boarding house. Jake was at the bottom of the steps, but the wagon wasn't there.

"One more stop," announced Jake, "the Riverton Hotel. David Acker would like you to be his guests for dessert. Just follow me."

Jake led them around the corner and into the Riverton Hotel, where he ushered them into the hotel's dining room. They unbuttoned their coats and admired the spread. There were two beautiful cakes, a large urn of coffee, and two pots of tea.

"My thanks to you for caroling today," said Mr. Acker. "You've made some of our old people very happy, especially Samuel. Please help yourselves and have a seat by the fireplace. I want to tell you about Samuel."

Mrs. Davis and Audrey cut and passed out cake while Wilma Sue poured coffee and tea. As they were served, the group took chairs near the fireplace and began eating. When everyone was seated, Mr. Acker went to the window, looked out for a moment, and then turned around to face the group.

"Let me tell you why Samuel is so important to me. I was in Chicago many years ago, half owner of a small hotel. My partner and I had some serious disagreements, and we resolved them by dissolving our partnership. My partner bought my share of the hotel, and I decided to go out west. On my way to the train station, a man accosted me with a pistol and demanded all my money, which I had in a money belt. I had no choice but to give him the proceeds from the partnership or die. As I was preparing to hand my money over to him, a stranger crossed the street with a long cloth wrapped item, pointed it at the thief, and told him to drop his gun. The thief refused and said that he'd shoot the stranger as well as me. Well, the stranger replied, that was fine with him, because he was going to count to three and then shoot the thief. The thief said the stranger was bluffing and that he didn't have a gun, whereupon the stranger quickly removed the cloth and showed him a shotgun. Then the thief argued that gun wasn't loaded and demanded the shotgun and the stranger's money, as well as my money. The stranger gave the thief the choice to live or die. He told the thief that he had been robbed and had his horse stolen a few years earlier in the Rocky Mountains, and that the thief had shot him in the leg and left him to die. This caused the thief to turn his head and look more closely at the stranger. I saw my chance and quickly pulled my derringer and shot him. A derringer is good only at a very close range, so my shot was off; it only creased the thief's hand, causing him to drop his gun. Without a gun and facing two men, one with a shotgun, the thief wisely turned and ran."

"That's quite a story," said Reverend Wesley. "You've never told me about that."

"Well, that stranger was Samuel," explained Mr. Acker. "It seems that my ex-partner had hired the thief, Duke Badger, to rob me right after he paid me for my half of the partnership. He told Duke I had the money in the money belt."

"Why didn't Samuel shoot Duke when he had the chance?" asked Father O'Brien.

David smiled and said, "The shotgun wasn't loaded. I thanked him for stopping the robbery and possibly saving my life. We talked and got along well and liked each other, so we decided to get dinner, and he told me about Riverton. Samuel had friends in Riverton and said that he was returning there the following week. Since Riverton had no hotel, I saw an opportunity. The rest is history."

There was more talk about Riverton, Samuel, and Duke Badger. David then shared a few interesting stories about some of his hotel guests over the years. The grandfather clock chimed, and several members of the group realized that they had been listening to him for over an hour.

"Excuse us, Mr. Acker; I didn't realize the time," said Brad. "We've got to get home."

Jake Jackson opened the door, and the group left the hotel. Sarah Davis, her son Chris, and Bob Black walked back to the boarding house. The rest headed for the wagon.

Brad and William went ahead to help the ladies onto the wagon. As they descended the hotel steps, Audrey slipped and started to fall down the steps, headfirst.

"Ahhh!" she screamed.

William turned around and saw her falling. He grabbed the handrail with his left hand and stretched his right arm out to grab Audrey as she hurtled toward the muddy street. As soon as he caught her, he pulled her to his chest, stopping her fall.

"Are you hurt?" he asked, peering into Audrey's wide eyes.

Audrey paused for a moment and stammered, "I don't think so."

"I'll hold your arm until you're sure you won't slip again," he said.

"Thank you." Audrey cautiously placed her feet on the boardwalk and reluctantly retrieved her arm from William's grasp.

"Audrey might have been hurt if you hadn't caught her," said Reverend Wesley.

"Yes," agreed Father O'Brien. "It's fortunate that you were there to catch her."

When the group was aboard the wagon, Jake gently slapped the reins and headed to the church. The carolers talked about the visitations they had made and the Christmas gifts the reverend had given people. When they arrived at the church, Reverend Wesley again thanked everyone for helping him. Buck Hodges mounted his horse and then helped Wilma Sue climb up behind him. They waved as they headed for Wilma Sue's house.

"Thanks for the Bible, Reverend," said William as he

climbed aboard the wagon with Jake Jackson for the short ride to the livery.

Reverend Wesley looked up to see Audrey's eyebrows raised in confusion. "I see you have some questions."

"Yes," said Audrey. "William seems like a nice man. I don't think he could be the arsonist."

"I agree," said Brad. "He doesn't appear to be full of hate. He seems to be genuinely nice."

"Most people are good," said Father O'Brien.

"Yes," said Reverend Wesley, "unless they take Satan's tempting path. If they don't get off that evil path, Satan becomes their master."

"Bob and I doubled up on William last night and today," confided Father O'Brien.

"In William, we saw a man that needed the Lord's guidance," added the reverend.

"Martha's cooking softened his hard shell," said Father O'Brien. "Then we took turns talking to him."

"I think we've put him on the Lord's path," said Reverend Wesley. "Now, it's up to him."

"I've got a question, unrelated to William," said Brad.

"Ask away," encouraged the reverend.

"David Acker doesn't come to church. He writes a big check to Bevins' General Store to help the Petrovs. He provides a hotel room, at no charge, for Father O'Brien. And the three of you appear to be old friends."

Reverend Wesley laughed and held up his hand to stop Brad's questions. "It really is quite simple," said the reverend. "David is a man of the cloth, just as Trevor and I are. He is a rabbi."

"A rabbi?" inquired Audrey.

"Yes," explained Reverend Wesley, "a Jewish rabbi.

He is somewhat similar to a minister or priest. He's one of Riverton's religious leaders."

"We work together doing the Lord's work to help the people of Riverton," continued Father O'Brien. "David Acker was one of the first men that Reverend Wesley introduced me to when I arrived in Riverton."

"Now I understand why you seem to be old friends," nodded Brad, mounting his horse.

"Yes," smiled Audrey as she mounted Blaze. "Say hello to Mrs. Wesley for us."

"See you Sunday," said Brad as they turned their horses toward home and clucked them to a trot.

CHAPTER 13
THE ARSONIST'S LETTER

Sunday, 2 January 1881: Brad met the buggy in front of the church. His father got down, and they helped the women out. Brad climbed into the driver's seat, clucked, and drove the horses toward the side of the church.

"Good morning, Bentons," said Reverend Wesley, opening the front door. "Come in. Father O'Brien has already warmed the church."

Mrs. Benton went to the piano and started playing prelude music. Mr. Benton talked with Jake Jackson about the upcoming addition to the church and the reverend's house. Audrey waited for Wilma Sue, who was coming up the steps of the church.

While Brad wrapped the horse's reins over the hitching rail, he saw the Hodges's buggy arrive and waited to talk to Buck. Buck tethered his horse and walked over to Brad.

"Morning, Buck," said Brad. "Happy New Year."

"Morning, Brad. Happy New Year to you, too."

"No new fires," said Brad. "I hope it stays that way."

"Me too," said Buck as they walked to the front of the Church. "Have you heard anything more about the arsonist?"

"Nothing," said Brad. "I'm worried that the next fire will kill someone."

They climbed the front steps of the church and entered the narthex. Wilma Sue saw them and waved them over.

"Happy New Year," she said.

"Happy New Year," replied Buck.

"Ma's playing the opening hymn," said Brad. "We'd better get seated."

The church service started as it always did. Reverend Wesley strode down the aisle on the second verse, turned to face his congregation, and continued singing. The reverend said the opening prayer, and a deacon read the designated scripture.

"Today's sermon is about forgiveness and love," said the reverend. "But first, I'd like to acknowledge the presence of Riverton's two Jewish families--the Ackers and the Petrovs. By the end of the service you'll understand why I invited them."

The sermon kept the congregation wholly engrossed and on edge as they listened to the reverend. When he finished, he reached into his pocket and pulled out some folded sheets of paper.

"I'll read a letter I received two days ago," he said. "I've already shared this letter with Sheriff Tate and our community's religious leaders -- Father O'Brien and David Acker." David Acker nodded in agreement.

He lifted the paper and began reading. "I am Duke Badger's son. I came to Riverton to avenge my father's death."

There was a murmuring of oohs through the Church.

Reverend Wesley waited for the murmuring to subside before continuing.

> "I attended your church to learn about the people responsible for my father's death. Most of you know that my father was attacked and killed by a wounded bear as the U.S. Marshals pursued him. The Marshals that pursued my father were John Abbott, Anthony Bevins, Henry Benton, and Ivan Petrov. I learned where these men lived, and then I burned the house of Vasya and Olga Petrov, set fire to the Bevinses' house, and burned old man Abbott's shack. I also set fire to the Bentons' house. I now know these were not the houses of the U.S. Marshals."

Reverend Wesley held the sheet of paper up for the congregation to see and said, "This man was consumed by hate. He was walking down one of Satan's tempting paths."

He turned the page and continued reading.

> "As a brief resident of Riverton, I danced with Audrey Benton, the daughter of the man my father shot. I met her brother, Brad, and the rest of the people in the church."

Audrey's mouth opened in shock at the revelation. There was another swell of whispers from the congregation. Brad looked at his sister in disbelief as their father put an arm on his daughter's shoulder. Mrs. Benton and Nana looked at each other. Nana dabbed her eye with a handkerchief while a tear trickled down Mrs. Benton's face, falling on a piano key. People sat up straighter and looked at their neighbors.

"Let me continue," said the reverend.

> "I sang Christmas carols and joined Reverend Wesley and Father O'Brien on their Christmas visitations. One of the elderly ladies we visited had been a passenger on the stagecoach that my father held up. She praised Brad and Audrey for bandaging the driver's wound, the result of a gunshot from my father. She expressed great admiration for Brad, who under Jim Bates' direction quickly learned how to drive a six-team stagecoach back to Riverton."

The congregation felt a blast of cold air from their left and looked over to see Father O'Brien closing the side door of the church. He nodded in agreement to what the reverend had just said.

> "When I returned from school in the East, I saw Sarah Davis, although she didn't see me. This woman had been enslaved by my father to help Blue Bird, an Indian woman, cook and keep house. Sarah was also required to provide medical treatment for my father and his men."

Reverend Wesley put the second page of the letter on his pulpit and commented, "His father had sent him away to school, and upon his return his father was killed. Understandably, though misguided, he sought revenge for his father's death. Then, the Christmas visitation presented him with a clear picture of what his father really was: an evil, sadistic man. He was confronted with the horror of what his own father had done to people. Put yourself in his shoes. Imagine his pain, the anguish of such a discovery."

Reverend Wesley picked up the letter and continued to read it.

> "Reverend Wesley, Father O'Brien, I must thank you for showing me the truth. I thank you for telling me about the Lord, and for telling me about forgiveness. And again, thank you for the Bible."

The reverend held up the letter and said, "This is forgiveness. He realized that he was on one of Satan's tempting paths."

Reverend Wesley with deliberateness picked up the last page and began reading.

> "Reverend Wesley, thank you for bringing me into your home on Christmas Eve. Thank you for showing me the true spirit of Christmas. Please forgive me for the pain that I caused the Petrovs, the Bevinses, Mr. Abbott, and the Bentons. I am truly thankful that you helped me stop feeding the fires

of revenge; that you helped me realize the futility of stoking the furnace of hate."

The reverend stopped reading, looked out at his congregation, and said, "The man who wrote this is no longer in Riverton. He doesn't feel he can face the people for whom he caused so much pain, people he almost killed."

Reverend Wesley found the last page and continued reading.

"Please forgive me for what I have done."

He folded the papers back up, placed it inside his jacket, and said, "The letter is signed William Brock, a new Christian."

Reverend Wesley turned toward the piano and said, "Abby, the closing hymn, please."

Mrs. Benton fumbled with the hymnal, dropping it on the floor. As she bent down to retrieve it, the reverend turned to the congregation and said simply, "Please forgive him."

Abby opened the hymnal and began playing the closing hymn. People quietly filed out of the church. After the closing hymn, Edith Bevins went to the front of the church, and put her arm around Mrs. Benton. Wilma Sue and Buck chatted with Brad and Audrey while Hank Lacy and Harold Benton talked in the narthex. As they left, everyone congratulated Reverend Wesley on the best sermon they had ever heard. Some folks called him a true hero for stopping the fires.

"I'll get the buggy, Pa," said Brad.

"Reverend," said Mrs. Benton. "It must have been horribly painful for William Brock to realize what his father really was."

"Yes, but he had the courage to face reality," said the reverend.

"I'm glad there won't be any more fires," she replied.

"Brad's here with the buggy," said Nana, putting her hand on her daughter's arm. "We'd best be going. See you next Sunday, Reverend. Thank you for a superb sermon."

Brad helped his mother and grandmother into the buggy, then stepped back as his father gently slapped the reins and headed home.

He climbed the front steps and re-entered the church. Audrey was speaking with Wilma Sue and the reverend.

"Do you realize that I danced with Duke Badger's son, and that he set fire to our house two weeks later?" said Audrey.

"You got to dance with the son of one of the most wicked outlaws in the country," said Wilma Sue. "Another one of your great adventures, and I lead a dull life helping my father in the general store."

"He saved you from a nasty fall too," said Buck. "Remember when you fell coming down the steps of the Riverton Hotel after the Christmas visitations?"

"Yes," sighed Audrey dazedly. "He grabbed me in mid-air and clutched me to his chest."

Wilma Sue tossed her hands into the air and wailed, "The son of Duke Badger holds you in his arms, and I just clerk at my father's general store. You get all the excitement."

"We all guided him away from Satan to the Lord's

path," said Reverend Wesley, putting his hands on Audrey and Wilma Sue's shoulders. "We did it together. Thank you."

"Audrey," said Brad after the reverend had gone back into the church. "Nana doesn't like us to be late for dinner. We'd better be going."

They slowly walked to their horses.

"Please help me up," said Audrey. "I'm too weak right now to do it alone."

Brad helped his sister mount her horse; then he mounted Ebony. They reined their horses around and headed north. The bright sun was overhead, melting the snow. Patches of green pine and fir trees contrasted with the glistening white snow and scrubby brown grass. As they reached the lane to their house, Brad stopped his horse. Audrey stopped Blaze and looked expectantly at her brother.

"I'll race you to the house for the last piece of Nana's pie," said Brad.

"Brad, you can have the last piece of pie and my piece of pie too. After the reverend's sermon and the letter, I'm too drained to race you."

ADDENDUM:
SOUSA

John Philip Sousa, the "March King," was the fourteenth leader of the United States Marine Corps Band. To many, his name is synonymous with America, the Fourth of July, and the United States Military. He is best known for his march, "The Stars and Stripes Forever."

Sousa was a prolific composer and an accomplished author. His musical works include 15 operas, 136 marches, 70 songs, and 11 suites for band. He published three novels, over 130 articles, and his autobiography, entitled *Marching Along, 1928*. He designed a tuba, known as the Sousaphone, specifically for marching.

He was born in Washington, DC on 6 November 1854. Sousa's primary instrument was the violin, but he also learned to play the trombone, baritone, and the cornet. In 1868, at the age of 13, he was old enough to serve as an apprentice, so he enlisted as an apprentice in the United States Marine Corps Band. He was discharged in 1875.

Sousa re-joined and took command of the United States Marine Corps Band in October 1880. The band at that time was comprised of approximately 40 men, primarily European musicians. Sousa discharged the less competent musicians and recruited professional musicians he knew from Philadelphia and Washington DC.

In the late 1800s, it was an unwritten requirement that U.S. Military bandleaders be Masons. Freemasons, more commonly known simply as Masons, is the name for a fraternal organization of men. It is based on the fatherhood of God and the brotherhood of man. While it is not a religious organization, it promotes the religious principles of friendship, charity, and kindness. It teaches its members to serve the Lord by helping others. Fourteen Presidents of the United States have been Freemasons, starting with George Washington. Thirteen signers of the U.S. Constitution were Freemasons as well. The Freemasons are not a secret society, and members are men from many nationalities, religions, and political parties. In Anglo-Saxon countries, however, membership consists primarily of white Protestants.

In keeping with this unwritten requirement, Sousa became a 3rd degree Mason in November 1881. He was a member of the same lodge as Congressman Garfield (soon to be President Garfield), with whom he felt a special Masonic kinship.

Sousa remained commander of the United States Marine Corps Band until he resigned in 1892 and formed his own band. Later in 1892, the death of a well-known composer and band leader, John Gilmore provided Sousa with the opportunity to hire 19 of Gilmore's players, including the famous Arthur Prior on trombone and Herbert L. Clarke on cornet. Sousa's band started with 46 players but by 1920 had grown to 70.

During World War I, Sousa was asked to join the U.S. Navy as a Lieutenant to train bandsmen at the Great Lakes Naval Training Center in Illinois. He did, but patriotically insisted that his pay be only one dollar a month. He took the training band, at times numbering 350 men, and toured major cities in the East and Midwest in support of the Red Cross, Navy Relief, and Liberty Loan Bonds. Sousa's battalion band sold over twenty-one million dollars in Liberty Loan Bonds. In January 1919, he returned to non-active duty, or civilian status while retaining his commission in the Navy. Shortly thereafter, he was promoted to the rank of Lieutenant Commander in the Naval Reserve.

John Phillip Sousa died on Sunday, 6 March 1932 of a heart attack in his sleep in Reading, Pennsylvania. Three days later, his body lay in state at the Marine Band Auditorium in Washington, D.C. The evening of 9 March, the United States Marine Corps Band participated in a memorial program, which was narrated by a young radio announcer, Arthur Godfrey. Godfrey later became a well-known entertainer during the golden era of radio. Sousa was buried with full military honors in the Congressional Cemetery on 10 March 1932. A Marine Corps bugler played "Taps."

An excellent biography of John Philip Sousa was written by Paul Bierley, who spent nine years researching his subject. Bierley's book is entitled *John Philip Sousa, American Phenomenon*, published by Prentice Hall, Englewood Cliffs, New Jersey, 1973.

ADDENDUM:
CHARLES DICKENS

Charles Dickens was born on the 7th of February 1812 in Portsea, just south of Portsmouth, England on the English Channel.

His father, John Dickens, was a clerk in the pay office of the Royal Navy. Although he handled money for the Royal Navy, he was, ironically, inept at handling his own money. In February 1824, when Charles was 12 years old, his father's debts caught up with him. John Dickens was sent to debtors' prison for failure to pay those debts. Debtors' prison was a typical punishment at that time for those who owed money and couldn't pay.

When his father went to prison, Charles was removed from school and sent to live in a workhouse for six shillings a week. This pay was the only income he had to support himself. Four months later, in May 1824, his father was released from prison. Charles returned to his family and was re-enrolled in a local school. At that time, schools were not supported by taxes, but by tuition paid by the students' parents.

Charles was an avid reader and had a very creative imagination. He read the works of Shakespeare, *Tales of the Arabian Nights*, and popular novels of the time.

He excelled in his studies during his last two years of school.

In 1827, at the age of 15, Charles completed school and became an office boy in the law firm of Ellis and Blackmore. While working there, he took it upon himself to learn shorthand, a skill which in 1831 enabled him to become a reporter for his uncle's newspaper, the *Mirror of Parliament*, and a year later a reporter for the *True Sun*. During this period, he wrote short fictional sketches based on life in London. In 1836, these short stories were published in a collection entitled *Sketches by Boz*.

His first novel, *Pickwick Papers*, was published in serial form, with a new chapter published each month beginning in April 1836. *Pickwick Papers* brought him fame and launched his writing career.

In January 1842, he began a six-month tour of the United States. Charles was quite outspoken about copyright laws and slavery in the U.S. Slavery was a volatile issue before the Civil War, and his opinions brought him an abundance of negative comments in the U.S. newspapers. When he returned to England, Dickens wrote his next novel, *Martin Chuzzlewit*. This was a satire on American characteristics, also published in serial form.

He started *A Christmas Carol* in the latter half of October 1843 and completed it in early December. He wrote the book on commission, meaning he would only earn a small royalty for each book sold. Since his payment would only be a percentage of the sales price, Dickens wisely had the book bound in red cloth and gilded the edges to make it attractive enough to bring a good price. The book also included four-color etchings, as well as and black and white etchings, to lure readers. *A Christmas Carol* sold well and increased his popularity.

His novels *Oliver Twist* and *Nicholas Nickleby* established Dickens as a social reformer in England. He worked with two well-to-do women on social projects such as clearing slums, creating schools for poor children, and helping homeless and "fallen" women. A recurring theme in his writing was the depiction of people controlled and exploited by businesses and banks.

Although his last years were professional successes, his personal life was a failure. Due to his affair with a young actress, his wife left Charles and went to live with their oldest son. With the tumultuousness of his personal life, his health deteriorated.

Aside from causing his marriage to fail, his personal ethics remained those of a Christian. Because Dickens worked for social reform to eliminate the cruel and dehumanizing actions of society's institutions at that time, the followers of Karl Marx tried to make him their spokesman. While his social reform goals were similar to the ideals of the Marxists and Socialists, his commitment to his Christian faith was not compatible with them.

Charles Dickens died on June 9, 1870, having completed six of the 12 chapters of his last novel, *The Mystery of Edwin Drood*. He was buried at Gad's Hill, England; his death was mourned by much of the English-speaking world.

ADDENDUM:
HARK! THE HERALD ANGELS SING

Reverend John Wesley was the founder of the Methodist Church. His younger brother, Reverend Charles Wesley (1707 – 1788), was a prolific hymn writer, producing about 6,500 hymns during his life. The text of his hymn, *Hark! The Herald Angels Sing*, first appeared in print in *Hymns and Sacred Poems (1739)*. The text was slightly modified during the next 14 years until it reached its present form, as published in George Whitefield's *Collection of 1753*. Despite the variations, the text is still primarily that of Charles Wesley.

Felix Mendelssohn (1809–1847) was born into the Jewish faith. Since music in 19th century Germany was centered on Christianity, however, Mendelssohn's father realized that being a Jew would severely limit Felix's musical opportunities. Thus, the father converted the family to Christianity.

In 1840, Felix was commissioned to write music suitable for the 400th anniversary of Gutenberg's printing press. For the Gutenberg commemoration, Mendelssohn wrote, *Festgesang #7*, opus 68, for men's voices and brass instruments. Fifteen years later, the English musician William Cummings matched Wesley's text with the second chorus of Mendelssohn's work, creating what we know today as *Hark! The Herald Angels Sing.*

The setting of Wesley's text to Mendelssohn's music proved to be a match approved by the Christian world. As is often the case with great art, the carol is an ecumenical blending of Jewish, Catholic, Anglican, and Protestant contributions.

BRAD AND AUDREY
PLAN THE CAPTURE OF
AN ENTIRE GANG!

FOR AN EXCERPT, TURN THE PAGE.

CHAPTER 1
THE THEFT

"The first one to the corral gets the biggest piece of pie," challenged Audrey, reining Blaze to a halt.

"On the count of three," replied her brother, stopping his horse, Ebony, beside her.

The horses sensed the excitement of another race. Ebony bobbed her head, and Blaze gave a quick snort. The quarter-mile lane to the corral would go quickly. The spring sun invigorated the horses and their riders.

"One, two, three," counted Audrey loudly, leaning forward in her saddle. The horses bolted forward and galloped toward the corral gate.

"A tie," declared Brad, as Ebony stopped inside the corral. Instead of dismounting, he sat silently in the saddle, looking over at the house.

Looking over her saddle, Audrey teased, "If you stay on your horse, I'll eat both pieces of pie."

"The back door is open!" exclaimed Brad, dismounting slowly. "I know I closed it before we went to church."

"I know you did," confirmed Audrey, suddenly attentive to her brother's words, "because I checked it, too."

Leaving their horses in the corral, they went to the

back door. As they reached the open door, they heard their parents' buggy approach.

"We'd better wait for Pa," cautioned Brad.

"I'll get him," said Audrey, running to the buggy.

Audrey quickly explained what they had seen. Harold Benton jumped down, looped the reins over the corral rail, and ran to the back door with his daughter. They slowly entered the house; their father stopped, listened, and looked around the kitchen.

"The pie is missing," said Brad in a whisper.

"Nana's skillet and stew pot are missing, too," said Audrey.

Their father reached under his winter coat on the coat hook, removed his gun belt, and strapped it on. Drawing his pistol, he slowly walked into the parlor.

"No one is here," said Brad. "They probably robbed us while we were at church."

"I believe you're right, but I'll check upstairs anyway," replied his father.

A few minutes later, all five Bentons were in the kitchen talking about the robbery.

"The apple-blackberry pie, my best skillet, and the stew pot are gone," said Victoria, Brad and Audrey's grandmother. Nana, as they called her, had come to Riverton to help their mother just before Audrey's birth and had remained. Her husband had been killed in the Civil War.

"Check your rooms," ordered their mother. "If he, or they, took the pie and stew pot, they probably searched every room for valuables. After you've checked your rooms, we'll all meet here and talk about Sunday dinner."

Brad opened his chest of drawers, found everything

there, and then checked his closet, only to find that his new rifle was missing. "Pa, my rifle is gone."

"Harold," said his wife, "the gold locket you gave me at our wedding is missing."

"I don't think I'm missing anything," said Audrey.

"I'm not missing anything, either," said Nana. "The Bible my father gave me as a wedding present is the only thing of value that I have, and that is sentimental value. The thief, or thieves, certainly weren't looking for the word of the Lord."

"Let's discuss this at Sunday dinner, without the pie," said their father grimly.

Nana nodded at Brad, "bring up some vegetables. I'll make biscuits, since they also took the bread I'd baked. The roast is still in the oven. They smelled the pie and bread and ignored the roast."

"Amen," said their father, concluding the blessing.

"Don't let the burglary ruin our Sunday dinner," commanded Nana.

"I won't," said Brad.

Harold Benton cut slices of roast beef and placed a slice on the plate his wife, Abby, held. She passed the plate to Audrey, who passed it to Brad, who passed it to Nana. By the time he placed a slice on his own plate, the rest of the family had already helped themselves to the biscuits and vegetables.

"Nana," said Brad, "You were right when you said the thieves weren't looking for the word of the Lord, because they took a real mix of things: they took my rifle, a pie, Ma's locket, the new skillet, the stewpot, and the bread."

"It is an odd assortment, but logical," she observed. "The rifle and gold locket can be sold. They took the food because they were hungry, and the skillet and pot either because they needed them or because they can also be easily sold."

"Then they're probably new to the area," concluded Audrey.

"Or passing through," added their mother. "I hope they're passing through, I wouldn't want to have more things stolen."

"I'll talk to Sheriff Tate first thing Monday morning," said their father. "There is nothing he can do about the theft today. Brad and I looked but didn't find any unique horse or wagon tracks."

"A few weeks without rain make it hard to see any horse or wagon tracks, even unique tracks," added Brad. "I don't think even Running Bear could find the thief's tracks."

"Is the ground really that hard?" asked Audrey.

"It is on the road," confirmed Nana, as she saw Brad eat the last bite of roast from his plate. "The thief would have come down the lane to the house, not through the pasture. We destroyed his tracks when we came home."

"Pa, may I have another slice of roast?" Brad interrupted, passing his plate to his grandmother's waiting hand.

Nana added two biscuits to Brad's plate while Harold cut a thick slice of roast beef for his son.

"Thank you," said Brad, taking the plate.

She continued, "Everything that was taken is

replaceable. The skillet, pot, and rifle are easy to replace. The locket will be more difficult, but I'll ask Sheriff Tate to wire a description of it and its engraving to Denver. Denver is the closest place where they could sell jewelry."

"Harold," said Abby, her eyes moist, but with a strong voice. "I have you, despite Duke Badger's attempt on your life. The locket reminds me of our courtship and marriage, beautiful memories. But," her voice briefly quavered, then she continued firmly, "the memories are there forever, even without the locket."

Brad and Audrey said nothing as they studied their parents. Their memories of searching for their father last October, after the sheriff's posse had failed to find him, were indelibly imprinted in their minds.

"Henry took care of that, that beast!" spat Nana. "That despicable monster, Duke Badger, got just what he deserved."

Duke Badger had held up the stagecoach that Brad, Audrey, and their father were taking to Denver. When Duke discovered that the stage had no gold, he took their father with him. The next day Sheriff Tate and his posse began an unsuccessful three-day search. Brad and Audrey left the next day searching for their father on their own.

"I remember seeing two wolves drop dead in front of me," recalled their father. "I kept my eyes on the other wolves. When I saw two more wolves drop, I knew the help I had prayed for had arrived."

Duke had taken their father's hat, coat, and boots before wounding him. Then, laughing, Duke Badger had ridden off, leaving their father to the wolves.

"You taught us how to shoot, Pa," comforted Audrey, gripping her father's hand. "We aimed and gently squeezed the trigger, just like you told us."

"That was excellent marksmanship," confirmed Nana. "I believe it was half a mile."

"It wasn't that far," commented Brad, "It was only about 200 yards."

"It was over a quarter of a mile," corrected their father. "And," he paused, "it was starting to snow and the wind was blowing."

"We found you in time, Pa," said Audrey. "That is what really counts. We found you before the blizzard or the wolves got you."

"And we just missed tangling with Duke Badger," said Brad.

Brad and Audrey bandaged their father's wound and built a shelter as the blizzard was starting. Three days later, they rode into Riverton with their father and a member of Duke Badger's gang that they had captured.

"I'll talk to Buckley Hodges Monday about your rifle, Brad," said his father. "The thieves may try to sell it locally, and he has the serial number, since he sold it to me."

"Buckley?" asked Audrey.

"Yes," replied their father, "Buckley. Buck Jr. is getting to be a young man, and folks are confusing their names, so Mr. Hodges is asking everyone to call him Buckley, and his son, Buck."

"That will help," agreed Brad. "New people won't have to ask, 'Jr. or Sr.' It will eliminate the junior or senior question."

"If your rifle doesn't show up in a few weeks, we can

order another one," encouraged Audrey. "We have more than enough reward money in the bank."

"Yes, we can order another one," agreed their father.

"Enough of this talk about outlaws and thieves," announced Nana. "We need to clean the table, do the chores and you two need to do your homework. I think I'll bake another pie, too. I'd like a piece before I go to bed tonight, how about you, Brad?"

"I'll get the apples and blackberries from the cellar," said Brad, rapidly pushing his chair back from the table.

"I think that means he'd like some pie," laughed his mother, gently patting her son on the back as he left the table.

"Supper is ready," announced their mother. "Hot tea, coffee, milk, roast beef sandwiches, and two apple-blackberry pies."

After a brief grace, Audrey poured coffee for her father while Nana poured tea for everyone else. Brad wasted no time and immediately began devouring his sandwich.

"I made a second sandwich for you, Brad," said Nana. "I thought you might have an appetite after chopping all that wood and kindling."

"Thank you," replied Brad.

"Pa, do you think the thief, or thieves, will return?"

"No, Audrey, I don't think they'll come back. But we should start locking our doors. Riverton is growing, new people are moving into town, and more people are passing through."

"Everyone leaves their doors unlocked," said Abby.

"You never know when someone might need shelter or food."

"I found a note from Len Reno last month," confirmed their grandmother. "His horse had gone lame while he was hunting. He hadn't eaten for about a day and walked miles to reach our place. Our house was unlocked, as usual, so he made himself a big breakfast of eggs, bacon, coffee, and some bread. To get home, he borrowed Ebony. That afternoon he rode back on his other horse, returned Ebony, and gave us a large venison roast as a thank-you present."

"You let him give you a roast for the use of Ebony?" questioned Brad.

"I couldn't very well refuse, but in return, I did give him a pie to take home," Nana replied.

"Starting tonight, we'll start locking the doors when we leave," said their father. "I have no concern about Len Reno, or most other folks. I do have a concern about the unsavory element that can come when a town grows, and Riverton is growing."

"A growing town often attracts criminal behavior," nodded Nana.

"Can't the thief just kick in the door?" asked Audrey.

"Yes, but many thieves will stop when they find the door is locked. Rather than break a window or kick in a door, they'll just go to the next house."

"Brad, will you please bring in the pie?" asked Nana.

"Right away," He pushed his chair back and hurried to the kitchen.

"We'll use our sandwich plates," said their mother. "No need to use more dishes."

Brad placed the pie in front of his grandmother with a large knife.

"A very small slice for me, please," requested their mother. Give my young man the rest of my piece."

"Thank you, Ma."

Victoria cut the pie; she put a small slice on Abby's plate, and a large one on Brad's. "Thanks, Nana," said Brad as he took the plate.

"You're starting to get some meat on your bones," observed his grandmother. "I don't want the ladies at church to start wagging their tongues about how I'm starving my grandson."

"They won't say that," laughed Harold Benton.

"Not if you keep feeding him, he is a growing boy," said Mrs. Benton. "Tomorrow will be a busy day. The principal doesn't want us to expect less from the students just because Easter Vacation is coming. Miss Jones will ask for your homework first thing in the morning."

Brad and Audrey washed the dishes, and then did their homework. As darkness fell, they said good night to their parents and Nana, and climbed the stairs to their bedrooms.

"Let's talk," whispered Brad as they reached the door to his room.

Audrey followed him in and sat on the floor beside her brother's chest of drawers, her back against the wall. Brad sat on the floor, leaned against his bed, and put his hands behind his head looking thoughtful.

"You've got a plan brewing under that black hair of yours," she said. "What is it?"

"I thought we should talk to Buck, Harry, and Wilma

Sue before school tomorrow. Harry always comes up with something when we present him with a problem. Maybe we'll be able to get an idea about who the thief might be."

"Yes," said Audrey. "But I don't want to get involved in another expedition to catch a thief."

"Why not?"

"I'd like to spend this vacation, well, vacationing. Our last three of our vacations have been spent chasing outlaws."

"We caught them, didn't we?" exclaimed her brother.

"Well, yes."

"That's good, isn't it?"

"Yes, but I want to make a dress and read a book during Easter Vacation. I don't have time to do it while we're going to school."

"I won't ask for your help in catching the thief," said Brad, a twinkle in his eye, "unless I really need you. I promise."

"Brad," her blue eyes flashing angrily, "You . . . you . . . exasperate me sometimes. And this is one of those times."

"Then you'll help me ask the questions," confirmed Brad, his face breaking into a smile.

"Yes, and I'll even help you capture the thief, or thieves. I'll sew a new dress on weekends, or during the summer."

"Thank you! I knew I could count on you," he said, getting up and opening the door for his sister.

"I'll see you in the morning," she said, her anger gone.

"In the morning," he replied.

OTHER TITLES BY THIS AUTHOR

THE BIGFOOT GANG

CAPTIVE

FIERY BLIZZARD

ABOUT THE AUTHOR

Born and raised in the West, Smith grew up where many farmers still used horses to plow their fields. Steam engines were the norm for railroads, and a diesel locomotive was quite an event. He's now caught up with modern civilization.

After serving in the U. S. Air Force, he later worked as a teacher, professional musician, and federal employee. He has now settled down and lives in Virginia. You can find out more about him at www.edgsmith.com.

CONNECT WITH THE AUTHOR

Website:
www.edgsmith.com

Social Media:
www.facebook.com/edgsmith

ACKNOWLEDGEMENTS:

Many thanks to Liza Potter for enhancing clarity, editing for all that grammar stuff, and partnering with me to bring the Benton Series to fruition. And to Liza's daughter, Lauren, for the young adult assessment. Kathryn Boudreau, and her dog Daisy, for taking photos and providing encouragement. A special atta-girl for Susie Nunez's special skills in making the liner comments {jacket items (author bio, about paragraph) cover description} come alive.